A Dance of Deception

THE THUNDERBOLT SERIES
BOOK TWO

TRISHA FUENTES

ARDENT ARTIST BOOKS

A Dance of Deception
The Thunderbolt Series - Book 2

Copyright © 2024 by Trisha Fuentes
All rights reserved.

Book Cover and formatting provided by Trisha Fuentes
trishafuentes.com

No part of this book may be reproduced in any form or by any electronic or mechanical means, including information storage and retrieval systems, without written permission from the author, except for the use of brief quotations in a book review.

ISBN: 979-8-3302-2158-5 (Paperback)

Published by
Ardent Artist Books
www.ardentartistbooks.com

About Ardent Artist Books

Ardent Artist Books was established in 2008.

We publish modern and historical romances once a month!

For a complete list of our published books and books in development, please visit our website at:

https://ardentartistbooks.com/free-downloads

FREE DOWNLOAD
Updated Monthly!

Follow us on YouTube to see what new stories are on the horizon!

https://www.youtube.com/theardentartist

Like, Subscribe & Comment

LET'S CONNECT!

Fuel your love of fiction with exclusive content and captivating insights from Ardent Artist Books. Whether you crave the thrill of modern narratives or the timeless elegance of historical fiction, our newsletter delivers a curated selection straight to your inbox.

Plus, as a welcome gift, receive a FREE downloadable eBook:

"The Family Fix"

https://mailchi.mp/567874a61a56/aab-landing-page

Contents

Chapter 1	1
Chapter 2	11
Chapter 3	21
Chapter 4	31
Chapter 5	41
Chapter 6	51
Chapter 7	63
Chapter 8	71
Chapter 9	81
Chapter 10	87
Chapter 11	95
Chapter 12	105
Chapter 13	117
Chapter 14	125
Chapter 15	135
Epilogue	143
Acknowledgments	147
Win the Heart of the Duchess	149
Your Next Series	151
The Family Fix	155
About Trisha	157
Also by Trisha Fuentes	159

One

LONDON, ENGLAND, 1817

The sky over England was a tumultuous symphony of storm clouds. Rain fell in a relentless deluge, transforming the verdant landscape into a world drenched in water. Thunder bellowed its fury, echoing through the heavens and shaking the sturdy manor house to its very foundations. Each rumble was a wild symphony of nature's power, enough to send even the bravest of souls scurrying for shelter.

Lady Genevieve Sinclair, known fondly to her friends as Vivie, watched from her perch by the window as the rain battered the cobblestones of the courtyard below. Her keen blue eyes traced the creeks as they coursed down the pane, each droplet reflecting a world turned topsy-turvy by the storm.

She marveled at how rain, such an ordinary thing, could transform everything it touched. The once dry courtyard now held pools of water that shimmered with each flash of lightning, and the manicured gardens were bowed under the weight of the deluge. Even her reflection in the glass seemed distorted and alien amidst the rain's dance.

Outside, a cavalcade of carriages arrived, their grandeur diminished by nature's erratic whims. Drawn by magnificent horses who seemed somewhat perturbed by their watery predicament, each carriage was a testament to society's futile attempt to control an uncontrollable world.

The first carriage attempted to navigate through the muddy path leading to the manor house but found itself stuck fast. Its wheels spun helplessly, churning up muck and dirt in a fruitless struggle for traction. The driver cursed under his breath and dismounted with a resigned sigh, his shiny boots sinking into mud that seemed almost eager to claim him.

Genevieve watched with veiled amusement as more carriages arrived, only to share their predecessors' fate. Each grand vehicle, regardless of the pedigree of the horses or the status of their occupants, succumbed to the power of nature. The courtyard, usually a scene of genteel order, had descended into chaos.

Her lips twitched as she watched the flustered footmen scrambling to assist their masters and mistresses. Their usually impeccable uniforms were splattered with mud, their powdered wigs askew in the downpour. She found it all incredibly entertaining.

As she watched the unfolding drama, Genevieve couldn't help but reflect on how this storm mirrored her feelings. Just as the rain transformed the world outside her window, she felt a tumultuous storm brewing within her. The pressures of societal expectations weighed heavily on her heart, and she longed for freedom from those shackles.

Like the carriages stuck in the mud, she felt trapped in a life that offered little room for maneuver. She yearned for a love that transcended social status and wealth—a love as passionate and wild as the storm raging outside.

Yet, for now, she was content to watch from her window perch, taking solace in the storm's raw beauty and finding amusement in society's futile struggle against nature's will. Little did she know that this storm was just the beginning of a series of events that would change her life forever.

UNDER THE AMBER radiance of countless twinkling candles, the elite of the Regency era danced in a glistening waltz. Men, donned in their immaculately cut dinner jackets, moved with poise and conceit, their vests as vivid as peacock plumage. Women, clad in a plethora of silk and satin gowns, flitted and groomed, their giggles airy and empty.

Above them, a string quartet played, their bows drawing sweet music from the strings with practiced ease. The melody floated above the din, wrapping itself around each guest like a lover's caress.

Amidst this sea of glittering finery and forced merriment, Lady Genevieve Sinclair entered. She clung to her father's arm, her fingers tracing the familiar patterns on his brocade sleeve. Her gown, a soft azure that matched her eyes, swirled around her ankles as she moved with a grace that was part her own and part borrowed from years of careful instruction.

Her heart fluttered nervously in her chest like a trapped bird yearning for freedom. She had been to many such events before; the guests were familiar, their faces etched into her memory. But every time she stepped into a ballroom like this one, she felt like an actor stepping onto a stage. The air seemed too thick with expectation and judgment, the laughter too shrill, and the smiles too painted.

Genevieve had never been one to take kindly to confinement. Even as a child, she had been more at home in the wide-open fields surrounding her family's estate than in the gilded cages of London society. She had grown up reading poetry under the dappled shade of willow trees and sketching portraits by candlelight.

She was not made for this world of empty words and empty hearts.

Her father's warm and familiar voice pulled her from her thoughts. "You look beautiful tonight, Vivie," he said, using his affectionate nickname for her.

Genevieve offered him a wan smile. "Thank you, Papa," she replied, her gaze drifting across the room. It landed on a young couple engaged in a close dance, their bodies moving as one to the rhythm of the music. They were smiling at each other, their eyes sparkling with a light that seemed to originate from somewhere deep within them.

Genevieve's heart ached at the sight. That was what she yearned for—a profound and all-consuming love, a love that was more than just convenience or duty, a love that transcended societal norms and expectations.

But in this world of her birth, where marriages were made over tea tables and broken card tables, such love seemed like an impossible dream. The young men who vied for her attention were not interested in her dreams or her passions. They saw only the beautiful heiress, not the woman beneath.

She took a deep breath, pushing away the disquiet that threatened to overwhelm her. She was Lady Sinclair, the daughter of a respected Earl. She had been born into privilege and responsibility. It was her duty to marry well and secure her family's position in society.

But as she looked around the room at the faces that were both familiar and strange, she could not help but feel a pang of longing. She yearned for something more – something real and raw, something that would set her soul on fire.

As she stepped further into the grand ballroom on her father's arm, Genevieve held her head high. Her heart might be heavy with unspoken dreams and silent yearnings, but she was a lady of the Regency era.

Her heart was pounding in rhythm with the rich notes of the string quartet. The room's luxury, with its high gilded ceilings and magnificent chandeliers, was suffocating in its splendor. Around her, a kaleidoscope of silks and satins swirled as elegantly dressed nobles moved to the music, their laughter a haunting melody against the strains of the orchestra.

"Genevieve, do stand up straight," a stern voice chided from behind her. The voice belonged to her mother, Lady Margaret Sinclair. She was a regal woman with a gaze as sharp as the diamonds glittering around her neck.

"Your posture is essential for making a good impression," she continued, adjusting the pearls around Genevieve's slender neck. Her gaze swept over Genevieve, analyzing her like a general preparing for battle. "Remember what's at stake here, my dear."

Securing a suitable match for Genevieve was paramount to their survival in society and to retaining their estate. Two daughters, with no son or male cousin—the Sinclair lineage hanging on the balance of a male heir.

As she turned to face her mother, she saw her younger sister, Lady Elizabeth, standing behind them. Elizabeth was every bit as beautiful as Genevieve but carried an air of youthful exuberance that often led to laughter rather than lectures.

"Why so serious, Vivie?" Elizabeth asked, poking fun at her sister's somber expression. "You look as though you're about to walk into battle rather than a ballroom."

"Perhaps because they feel much the same to me," Genevieve replied dryly. The corners of Elizabeth's lips twitched upward into a playful smile as she stifled a laugh.

Genevieve looked back at her mother and nodded obediently. She knew well the gravity of her duty, yet it felt as though she was trading her heart for the sake of propriety.

Her gaze strayed across the ballroom, past the dazzling nobles and their polite laughter, to the grand windows framing the night sky. The stars twinkled with a freedom that seemed so far from her reach. She yearned for a love that was as profound and boundless as the night sky. But tonight, her dreams felt as distant as those celestial bodies.

"Mother," she said, turning back to Lady Margaret, "I understand my duty, but surely there is more to marriage than securing alliances and amassing wealth."

Her mother's stern expression softened for a moment. "There may be more, Genevieve," she said gently. "But we do not have the luxury of waiting for it."

The words hung in the air between them, a sobering reminder of their reality. As the string quartet struck up a new tune and the laughter around them grew louder, Genevieve felt an acute sense of loneliness. It was as if she stood on one side of a chasm, with her dreams on the other.

She gave her mother a slight nod and forced a smile onto her face. She would do her duty. She would dance and smile and make polite conversation. She would be the perfect lady her mother wanted her to be.

But as she stepped onto the dance floor, a piece of her heart yearned for more than this glittering world of duty and decorum—for a love that was more than an advantageous match—a love that was real, deep, and true.

Yet tonight, under the sparkling chandeliers and amidst the sea of silks and satins, that love seemed as elusive as a star in the vast night sky.

Two

Genevieve glided gracefully across the dance floor, following the lead of Lord Alfred Huntley, the third eligible bachelor she had been paired with that evening. Though he moved with precision, his hand firmly clasping hers as they stepped and spun in time with the music, his conversation lacked any real depth or spirit. He prattled on about the lineage of his hunting dogs and the prowess of his marksmanship, subjects that utterly failed to capture Genevieve's interest or attention.

As Lord Alfred droned on about the points of a prized pointer named Percival, Genevieve allowed her gaze to drift across the ballroom, observing the other couples on the dance floor. Many of the ladies had their heads bent demurely as they listened to their partners. However, Genevieve suspected their minds were occupied by more diverting thoughts than the monotony of polite conversation. How stifling it must feel, she mused, to have one's true sentiments and opinions confined within the strict rules of propriety.

Her eyes settled on Lady Emily Carlisle, dancing stiffly with Sir Howard Morris. Emily's smile was fixed, her responses clipped as Sir Howard whispered eagerly into her ear. Genevieve noticed how Emily angled her body away from his, subtly attempting to increase the distance between them. Yet Sir Howard seemed either not to see or not to care about Emily's obvious discomfort. Here again, the power dynamics were at play: the man asserting his will and privilege, the woman required to tolerate it with grace.

Genevieve's dismay must have shown on her face, for Lord Alfred paused mid-sentence to ask with concern, "My lady, are you quite alright?"

"Yes, thank you," Genevieve replied automatically. "I fear the heat of the room has caused a slight dizziness. Would you be so kind as to fetch me a refreshment?"

Lord Alfred bowed. "It would be my honor." He guided her politely to the edge of the dance floor before striding purposefully towards the refreshment table, no doubt eager to escape her company.

Alone for a moment, Genevieve fanned herself lightly with her lace fan, more for appearance than any actual discomfort. As she surveyed the room, her eyes were drawn to a dark, striking figure standing near the French doors leading to the terrace. Though nearly everyone else was paired off for the dances, he stood apart, aloof and solemn.

Something about the man's proud bearing and the smoldering intensity of his gaze as he watched the dancing couples made Genevieve catch her breath. She quickly lowered her eyes, unsettled by the visceral pull she felt toward this brooding stranger. When she dared to look again, she found his piercing dark eyes fixed on her, causing a fiery blush to bloom on her cheeks.

"Your refreshment, my lady," Lord Alfred proclaimed grandly as he returned, proffering a crystal cup of punch.

Genevieve accepted it with murmured thanks, taking a small sip of the tart liquid. As Lord Alfred launched back into his monologue about prizewinning pointers, Genevieve's attention remained acutely focused on the tall, dark figure across the room. He had turned his back to her now, gazing out into the night, his very stillness conveying a power and magnetism that seemed to call to her.

"My lady?" Lord Alfred inquired, and Genevieve realized she had missed his question entirely. "Forgive me, my thoughts were elsewhere for a moment," she said. "You were saying?"

Lord Alfred huffed slightly but repeated himself: "I asked if your dance card is full this evening?"

Genevieve considered him for a moment. Though rather self-absorbed, he did not seem cruel or malicious like some of the other gentlemen present. "Yes, I'm afraid my card is quite full," she answered gently. Lord Alfred's face fell.

"But," Genevieve added, taking pity on him, "I would be happy to reserve you a dance at the next ball." Lord Alfred's expression immediately brightened. "You honor me, my lady," he said fervently, bowing over her hand as the music ceased.

As he retreated into the crowd, Genevieve saw her mother bearing down on her, steely determination in her eyes. "You must dance the next set with the Duke of Crowley," Lady Margaret commanded once she drew near. "With his wealth and connections, he would make a fine match."

Genevieve glanced over to where the Duke stood, red-faced and swaggering, one hand wrapped possessively around the waist of his frightened-looking dance partner. Revulsion rose in Genevieve's throat.

"Mama, you know the Duke and I have nothing in common," she protested. "Surely we could find a more suitable..."

But Lady Margaret would brook no argument. "It is your

duty to this family to make an advantageous match," she said sharply. "Now go, the next dance is starting."

With a resigned sigh, Genevieve allowed her mother to lead her across the floor to where the Duke awaited. As he pulled her roughly into hold, the cloying scent of brandy washed over her. Genevieve stiffened, steeling herself as the Duke leered down at her. This was her fate, and she realized despairingly that she was to be passed from man to man, valued only as a political pawn or pretty object.

Unless... her eyes darted back to where the dark stranger had been, but the spot by the terrace doors was empty now. Disappointment pierced her, though she knew not why she felt such a profound connection to a man whose name she did not even know. But perhaps that was the allure - here was someone who saw her as she indeed was, not merely a prize to be claimed.

As the Duke slurred vulgarities into her ear, Genevieve closed her eyes and allowed herself to slip into a daydream. She imagined herself back in the stranger's heated gaze, drawn to his body and soul. Indeed, such raw, instinctive attraction hinted at love without bounds or reason. It was this love she yearned for, no matter how wild or impossible —a love to set her free.

The music ceased, and Genevieve curtsied hastily to the Duke before withdrawing from his grasp. She needed air to clear her head and steady her nerves. Weaving through the crowd, she slipped out onto the terrace into the cool night. Laying her hands on the cold stone balustrade, she took a deep, fortifying breath. Above her, the inky sky glittered with stars, their tranquil beauty soothing her restless spirit.

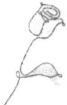

THE AIR OUTSIDE on the balcony was cool, a welcome relief from the stifling heat of the ballroom. Lady Genevieve Sinclair stood alone, her hands lightly gripping the ornate wrought-iron railing as she gazed at the London skyline. The lights from the grand mansion behind her danced across the surface of the river Thames, their reflections twinkling like a thousand stars in the inky water.

The solitude was intoxicating, a stark contrast to the muffled hum of music and laughter that seeped through the balcony doors. The sweet scent of roses wafted up from the garden below, adding to her sense of calm.

A sudden rustle from behind shattered her reverie. Turning around, she found herself face to face with a man she hadn't seen before. His brown hair fell casually over his forehead, just touching his blue eyes that sparkled with an unspoken mystery. He was dressed impeccably in an elegant black coat and cream-colored waistcoat that accentuated his tall and imposing figure.

"I apologize if I've intruded upon your solitude, my lady," he said, giving her a slight bow. His voice was rich and warm, resonating with an underlying strength that caught her off guard.

She tilted her head slightly, curiosity piqued by this stranger who had so suddenly appeared. "I don't believe we've been introduced."

A captivating smile graced his lips as he extended his hand towards her. "Alexander Hartfield, at your service."

"Viscount Hartfield?" she asked, recognition lighting up her eyes. She'd heard whispers about him - tales of his travels abroad and his passion for art and literature. Yet those stories did little justice to the man standing before her.

"The very same," he replied with a nod.

Intrigued by this enigmatic Viscount, who shared her interests in art and poetry, she decided to engage him in conversation. "Tell me, Viscount Hartfield, what brings you out here? Have the festivities inside become too much for you as well?"

He laughed softly, the sound filling the air with an unspoken charm. "I've always found that the most interesting conversations happen away from the crowds," he replied, his gaze meeting hers with a spark of shared understanding.

For the rest of the evening, they engaged in a lively exchange of thoughts and ideas, their conversation flowing as smoothly as the river below. They spoke of art and literature, of their dreams and aspirations. Despite his noble title, Viscount Hartfield spoke with a passion and sincerity that transcended societal boundaries, his words revealing a depth of character that intrigued her.

Genevieve found herself drawn to his enigmatic personality. His wit matched her own, and their shared interests made their conversation both enjoyable and enlightening. As they conversed, she noticed the way his eyes lit up when he spoke about art and poetry. She was captivated by his enthusiasm and the way he described his travels with such vivid detail.

As she listened to him speak, Genevieve felt a sense of connection she hadn't felt before. This was not the superficial chatter that dominated most social gatherings; this was a genuine exchange of ideas between two individuals who appreciated each other's intellect.

When it was time for her to return to the ballroom, Genevieve found herself reluctant to leave. She glanced at Viscount Hartfield, a spark of excitement igniting within her at the prospect of getting to know him better.

"May I call on you, Lady Genevieve?"

She offered him a small smile before turning away. "Until we meet again, Viscount Hartfield."

As she walked back into the grand ballroom, she couldn't help but feel a sense of anticipation for what lay ahead. For the first time in many social gatherings, she had met someone who intrigued her, someone who sparked her curiosity and matched her wit.

Viscount Alexander Hartfield was not just another nobleman. He was a mystery waiting to be unraveled, a book waiting to be read. And Lady Genevieve Sinclair was more than willing to turn the pages.

Three

The following day, Genevieve eagerly awaited the Viscount's arrival. She had received his letter to call on her, and she had spent the morning in a state of pleasant anticipation. Her thoughts drifted to the previous evening's encounter, and his charming smile, intelligent conversation, and ability to make her laugh had left an undeniable impression on her.

When the Viscount's carriage finally pulled up to the Sinclair residence, Genevieve's heart skipped a beat. She quickly smoothed her skirts and rushed to the drawing room, her cheeks flushed with excitement. As he entered, Genevieve was struck by his handsome appearance once more. His dark hair was neatly styled, and his blue eyes sparkled with intelligence and warmth. He was dressed in a tailored morning coat that accentuated his broad shoulders and lean physique.

The Viscount greeted Lady Margaret with a polite bow and a charming smile. "Lady Margaret, it is a pleasure to make your acquaintance."

Lady Margaret returned his greeting with a nod, her expression carefully neutral. "Viscount Hartfield, the pleasure is all mine."

Lord Sinclair stepped forward, extending his hand. "Hartfield, welcome to our home. We are honored to receive you."

The Viscount firmly shakes Lord Sinclair's hand. "Thank you, Lord Sinclair. I am delighted to be here."

Lady Elizabeth, unable to contain her excitement, curtsied deeply. "Viscount Hartfield, it is a true honor to meet you. I have heard so much about you from my sister."

The Viscount chuckled softly. "I am flattered, Lady Elizabeth. I trust your sister has not painted me in too favorable a light?"

Lady Elizabeth giggled. "Oh, no, Viscount. Genevieve has nothing but the highest praise for you."

The Viscount turned to Genevieve, his eyes meeting hers briefly. A warm smile played on his lips, and Genevieve felt a flutter in her heart.

"Shall we adjourn to the drawing-room?" Lord Sinclair suggested. We can have some tea and continue our conversation there."

Everyone agreed, and they made their way to the drawing room. Genevieve and the Viscount sat down on a settee while the others took their places in chairs nearby. A servant entered with a tea tray and poured everyone a cup.

From Genevieve's perspective, the Viscount seemed to make a favorable impression on her family. Her father engaged him in a lengthy conversation about politics and economics while her mother inquired about his family and estate. Lady Elizabeth chattered excitedly about the latest gossip and fashion trends.

Genevieve listened attentively, observing the Viscount's interactions with her family. He was charming, intelligent, and had a disarming sense of humor. He seemed to enjoy their company genuinely, and they, in turn, appeared to be smitten with him.

Genevieve couldn't help but feel a sense of unease amidst the growing admiration for the Viscount. While she found him attractive and charming, she couldn't shake the feeling that there was something beneath the surface that she couldn't quite put her finger on.

His gaze often lingered on her a bit too long, and his compliments, while flattering, felt calculated. She couldn't help but wonder if his interest in her was genuine or if he was playing a role to gain her family's favor.

Genevieve knew one thing for sure: she was comfortable with the Viscount.

As the afternoon wore on, Genevieve found herself increasingly at ease in the Viscount's company. Their conversation flowed effortlessly, punctuated by moments of witty banter and easy laughter. He had a knack for putting her at her ease, for coaxing her more reticent nature into cheerful engagement.

When talk turned to poetry, they discovered a mutual love for Lord Byron's romantic works. The Viscount quoted a passage of *Childe Harold's Pilgrimage* that vividly evoked the beauty of a moonlit Venetian night. Genevieve was enthralled by the imagery and the passion in his voice as he recited the verses.

"You have a true appreciation for the artistry of language," Genevieve said, impressed by the Viscount's knowledge and discernment.

"As do you, my lady," he replied warmly. "I confess I find such openness to beauty and imagination lamentably rare in polite society."

Genevieve nodded in agreement. "Yes, many seem to dismiss the world of arts and letters as frivolous. But I believe it offers a window to truth and meaning that bare facts cannot provide."

The Viscount regarded her thoughtfully. "You have an insightful mind, Lady Genevieve. I find myself quite captivated by your perspective."

Genevieve blushed at the compliment. She wasn't used to such open appreciation of her intellect and opinions. With the Viscount, she felt free to voice her thoughts without fear of censure.

As the afternoon waned, Lady Margaret delicately suggested a tour of the Sinclair mansion. The Viscount readily agreed, his blue eyes twinkling with genuine interest. But it was Lady Elizabeth who unexpectedly suggested that Genevieve be their guest's guide.

"Genevieve knows the mansion best," she stated, her eyes gleaming with mischief. "She can share the stories behind each portrait and antique."

Lord Sinclair chuckled heartily at his youngest daughter's impromptu plan, patting her on the shoulder in approval. "An excellent suggestion, Lizzy."

Lady Margaret, despite her initial surprise, gave a curt nod of agreement. She trusted Genevieve to conduct herself appropriately.

Genevieve felt a thrill of gratitude for her sister's unexpected intervention and the chance to be alone with the Viscount. She cast a quick, thankful glance towards Elizabeth, who returned it with a conspiratorial wink.

As they began their stroll through the mansion, Genevieve found herself relaxing in the role of tour guide.

"Your father tells me you have quite an affinity for art," he began, his voice smooth and captivating. His gaze shifted to a painting hanging above the mantelpiece. "This piece, for instance. I believe it's a Turner."

Genevieve followed his gaze to the painting - a mesmerizing landscape depicting a fiery sunset over rolling hills. "Yes," she replied, her blue eyes shining with admiration. "I find Turner's use of light and color absolutely fascinating."

Their conversation flowed like a gentle river - unhurried yet engaging. They spoke of art and poetry, and their shared passions created an immediate bond between them. But as the morning wore on, it wasn't just Hartfield's intelligence or his knowledge of art that drew Genevieve to him; it was also the glimpses of vulnerability that lay hidden behind his charming smile.

As Hartfield spoke about his travels across Europe - visiting museums and galleries - his eyes took on a distant look. It was as if he were standing on those cobblestone

CHAPTER THREE

streets again, the echo of foreign tongues in his ears and the taste of exotic foods on his lips. Genevieve couldn't help but feel a pang of sympathy for the man before her. Beneath the surface of this well-traveled, well-educated nobleman, she sensed a man yearning for something more - something she longed for - a love that transcended societal norms.

In that shared understanding, an unspoken connection was forged. Their laughter filled the room, bouncing off the high ceilings and reverberating in the air around them. But it was their silences that spoke volumes - comfortable and filled with unspoken words, laden with shared sentiments and secret dreams.

Hartfield's blue eyes held a depth of emotion that surprised Genevieve. They weren't just the eyes of a charming Viscount but those of a man who had seen much of the world yet still searched for something elusive.

In one particularly poignant moment, their conversation lulled, and Hartfield glanced at Genevieve, his gaze softening. "I must confess," he said quietly, "I've not met many who share such a deep appreciation for art and poetry."

"And I," she responded with a warm smile, "have not met many who understand why one might value such things."

For a fleeting moment, their eyes locked, and an unspoken understanding passed between them. They were two souls yearning for something beyond their reach—beyond societal expectations and family duties. This moment of shared vulnerability only deepened Genevieve's intrigue about this enigmatic Viscount.

She led the Viscount through grand halls adorned with portraits of her ancestors, past rooms filled with exquisite furniture from far-off lands, and into the library – her favorite room in the house.

The walls were lined with mahogany shelves laden with books of every genre and subject imaginable. The air smelled of aged paper and leather bindings, a scent that had comforted Genevieve in moments of solitude and introspection. As she entered, she couldn't help but breathe in deeply, closing her eyes for a moment to savor it.

Upon opening them again, she found Viscount Hartfield watching her with an intrigued smile. "You favor this room above all others," he observed, his voice softer now that they were alone.

Genevieve nodded. "Yes," she admitted. "This is my sanctuary. Each book is a portal to another world – worlds where women can be explorers, scholars, and adventurers."

Viscount Hartfield's eyes roamed over the shelves with an appreciative gleam. "I can see why you cherish this room,"

CHAPTER THREE

he said. "There is a wealth of knowledge here that could rival any man's library."

They continued their exploration, Genevieve pointing out the various pieces of art and explaining their history. The Viscount listened attentively, asking insightful questions that made her reconsider some of the things she'd taken for granted.

As they moved through the mansion, Genevieve couldn't help but appreciate the Viscount's easygoing demeanor. He seemed genuinely interested in her family's history and her interests. His thoughtful questions and observations showed a depth of character that was rare among the men of her acquaintance.

In these private moments with him, away from prying eyes and societal expectations, Genevieve found herself drawn to the Viscount in a way she hadn't anticipated. He was more than just a charming nobleman—he was a man who saw her as an equal and valued her thoughts and opinions.

As they strolled through the gardens to conclude their tour, Genevieve felt a sense of contentment wash over her. This afternoon, she revealed facets of Viscount Hartfield that she hadn't expected to find – facets she found increasingly attractive. And for the first time in many months, she found herself looking forward to what tomorrow might bring.

Four

The second week of the London Season was well underway, and the ballrooms were once again filled with a glittering array of available beauties and eligible bachelors. Genevieve and her mother, Lady Margaret, were among the attendees, their presence eagerly anticipated by the *ton*. As they entered the grand ballroom, all eyes turned towards them, their arrival causing a ripple of excitement through the crowd.

Genevieve, resplendent in a gown of shimmering emerald that accentuated her vibrant eyes, drew admiring glances from every corner of the room. She had become accustomed to such attention, yet it never failed to fill her with a sense of unease. She yearned for more than just admiration; she longed for a connection that transcended the superficial.

As Genevieve and her mother made their way through the crowd of guests, she caught sight of a familiar face. Viscount Hartfield stood near the edge of the dance floor, his gaze fixed upon her. A surge of anticipation coursed through Genevieve as he approached, his smile conveying both warmth and a hint of mischief.

"My Lady," he greeted her with a slight bow, his voice as smooth as velvet, "may I have the honor of this dance?"

Genevieve hesitated for a moment before accepting, her heart pounding with a mixture of excitement and trepidation. As they took to the dance floor, the music seemed to fade into the background, their focus solely on each other. They moved with effortless grace, their bodies responding instinctively to the rhythm.

With each step, Genevieve felt a growing connection with the Viscount. His conversation flowed effortlessly, revealing a depth of knowledge and wit that she found both captivating and refreshing. As they danced, she found herself drawn into his world, forgetting the stifling expectations of society and the superficiality that had come to define her existence.

After a few dances, Genevieve asked the Viscount for a reprieve. The ballroom was stifling, and she longed for a breath of fresh air. Viscount Hartfield readily agreed, and they stepped out onto the terrace.

CHAPTER FOUR

The night air was cool and refreshing, and the stars twinkled above them like a thousand tiny diamonds. Genevieve breathed deeply, savoring the peace and tranquility of the moment. She turned to face the Viscount, her eyes sparkling with a mixture of excitement and anticipation.

"Would you care to take a stroll?" he asked, his voice soft and inviting.

Genevieve hesitated for a moment before nodding. She had never walked alone with a man before, but she felt an inexplicable trust in the Viscount. Together, they walked through the gardens, their footsteps echoing in the silence of the night.

The sweet scent of blooming roses wafted through the air, mixing with the fantastic night breeze and carrying away the stifling memories of the dinner table.

Viscount Hartfield, ever the gentleman, offered his arm. Genevieve accepted, allowing him to guide her along the gravel paths that wound through the garden like intricate lacework. A thousand stars shone overhead, casting an ethereal glow on their surroundings and making the flowers glisten as though kissed by morning dew.

The Viscount's stride was measured, matching her own pace with ease. His silence was comfortable rather than imposing. Genevieve stole glances at him from beneath her lashes, taking in his handsome profile highlighted by the starlight. She found herself drawn to his calm demeanor amidst the whirlwind of societal obligations.

As they meandered past rows of rose bushes and flowering vines, Genevieve felt a sense of peace wash over her. The world beyond these garden walls, with its endless games of status and wealth, seemed a distant memory. Here, in this moonlit sanctuary, she could be Genevieve – not Lady Sinclair or an eligible maiden but a woman yearning for authenticity and understanding.

"I've always found solace in gardens," Viscount Hartfield said suddenly, his voice low yet apparent in the quiet night. "There's something comforting about their constancy."

Genevieve looked up at him, surprise flickering across her features. "I share your sentiments," she confessed. "The hustle and bustle of society can be quite overwhelming at times."

His blue eyes met hers in understanding. He nodded once before turning his gaze back to the path. "It's an endless game of cat and mouse. One that we are compelled to play regardless of our desires."

Genevieve couldn't help but agree. She'd felt the same frustration countless times before, the weight of societal expectations bearing down on her like a leaden shroud. It was a rare occurrence to find someone who shared her perspective.

"Viscount Hartfield," she began, her voice tentative yet determined. "I've often wondered if there are others like us who yearn for something beyond these societal games."

His gaze shifted back to her, contemplative. He considered her question for a moment before replying, "I believe there are more than we realize, Lady Sinclair. It's simply that they, too, are caught in the web of societal expectations."

As they continued their stroll beneath the starlit canopy, Genevieve felt a connection forming between them – a mutual understanding born out of shared disillusionment and yearning. It was as though they were two kindred spirits navigating the turbulent seas of Regency society.

Their conversation meandered as aimlessly as their path through the garden. They spoke of art and literature, shared stories of their childhoods, and even delved into their hopes and dreams. All the while, the night bloomed around them in a symphony of nocturnal melodies and fragrant blossoms.

It was an evening Genevieve would remember not for its grandeur or luxury but for its simplicity and authenticity. For the first time in what felt like an eternity, she felt seen – not as a pawn in society's game but as a woman with dreams and desires of her own.

As they made their way back to the mansion arm in arm, Genevieve couldn't help but glance at Viscount Hartfield with renewed interest. Beneath his noble title and handsome exterior lay a man who was just as disillusioned with society as she was—a man who sought authenticity in a world of pretense.

In Viscount Hartfield, she found a kindred spirit – a beacon of understanding in a sea of conformity. And in that realization, she felt a spark of hope ignite within her heart. Perhaps, just perhaps, she wasn't alone in her quest for a love that transcended societal expectations.

AMIDST THE VIBRANT tapestry of the ballroom, Genevieve found herself momentarily alone. The Viscount had been whisked away by another family eager to introduce their eligible daughter to the charming nobleman. Genevieve watched as he disappeared into the crowd of people, a flicker of disappointment crossing her features.

Her sapphire eyes flickered across the room, observing the men and women who made up the upper crust of London's society. A riot of colors danced before her eyes, a swirl of silks and satins, laces and brocades. Her ears filled with a cacophony of laughter, whispers, and the enchanting melody of the string quartet nestled in a corner.

When she began to feel the weight of loneliness settled upon her, a voice broke through her reverie. "May I have this dance, Lady Genevieve?"

She turned to find a young man with sandy hair and a charming smile extending his hand towards her. Genevieve hesitated for a moment before placing her hand in his. As they moved gracefully across the dance floor, she couldn't help but compare him to the Viscount. This man, though pleasant enough, lacked the enigmatic charm and intelligence that had so captivated her earlier.

Despite the luxury that surrounded her, Genevieve felt an overwhelming sense of confinement. The societal elite gathered in the room were nothing more than gilded cages to her. They were bound by rigid expectations and etiquette, forced to wear masks of civility even as they partook in frivolous conversations and petty rivalries.

She was pulled onto the dance floor by yet another hopeful suitor. As she danced with him, her hand delicately placed in his while her other hand rested lightly on his shoulder, she felt a pang of disillusionment. Their movements were synchronized, but their minds were far from harmony. He spoke with an air of self-importance about his recent ventures and investments while she responded with polite nods and noncommittal hums.

The conversation was as monotonous as the steps they traced on the polished marble floor. It was like a rehearsed play where everyone knew their lines but lacked genuine emotion. Genevieve yearned for more than this superficial dance, both literally and metaphorically.

After a seemingly endless round of dances with suitors who saw her more as a prize to be won rather than a woman to be understood, Genevieve sought solace at the fringes of the ballroom. She took a moment to adjust her delicate pearl necklace before casting her gaze around once more. Her eyes searched for the Viscount, but he was nowhere to be found.

She watched young debutantes flutter their fans flirtatiously at dashing gentlemen, mothers eyeing potential matches for their daughters, and old friends exchanging news and gossip. She observed the orchestrated spectacle, the veiled alliances, and the strategic social maneuvers that made up the dance of the aristocracy.

As she watched, she couldn't help but feel a growing sense of disillusionment. These interactions were so calculated, so devoid of genuine warmth and understanding. *Where was the depth, the connection that was supposed to transcend societal ranks and material wealth?*

A soft sigh escaped her lips as she longed for someone who could see beyond her title and beauty. Someone who could understand her passion for art and poetry and her desire to live life on her terms. Someone who could see the fire that burned in her eyes when she spoke about things that truly mattered to her.

But such men seemed to be in short supply in these circles. It was all about status, wealth, and power. The suitors that surrounded her were interested in securing their lineage or increasing their wealth through a favorable marriage. Few, if any, seemed to be interested in love or companionship.

Genevieve yearned for more. She longed for love as passionate as the poetry she cherished, as vibrant as the paintings she admired, a love that transcended societal norms and expectations, a love as real and raw as life itself. *Was the Viscount such a man?*

As another hopeful suitor approached her with a practiced smile on his face, Genevieve prepared herself for yet another dance, yet another conversation filled with flattery and hollow promises.

Genevieve was not just an eligible match or a beautiful woman; she was a spirited soul yearning for a love that was profound, genuine, and timeless. And she would not rest until she found it.

Five

The third week of the London Season had arrived, and Lady Andrews' Masquerade Ball was the talk of the town. The most eligible bachelors in England would be in attendance, their faces hidden behind masks, their identities a compelling mystery. Young beauties fluttered their fans and whispered excitedly, their hearts pounding with anticipation.

Genevieve, accompanied by her mother, entered the grand ballroom, her gaze sweeping across the sea of masked figures. The air crackled with excitement and intrigue. She longed to experience the freedom and anonymity that the masquerade offered, to lose herself in the crowd and dance the night away without the constraints of society's watchful eyes.

But as she searched for a familiar face, a pang of disappointment washed over her. Viscount Hartfield was nowhere to be seen. She had hoped to share this evening with him, to lose herself in their conversations and forget the superficiality of the Season. Without him, the ball seemed to lose its luster, becoming just another obligation she had to endure.

Genevieve's gaze drifted across the ballroom, searching for a distraction from her disappointment. Suddenly, her eyes were drawn to a figure standing in the shadows, his presence commanding attention. He was tall and fit, his broad shoulders hinting at hidden strength. His mask concealed his features, but his piercing gaze seemed to see right through her.

He moved with an air of confidence and secrecy, his every step radiating an aura of danger and intrigue. Genevieve felt an inexplicable pull towards him as if fate had brought them together in this crowded room. She longed to know who he was, to unravel the secrets hidden behind his mask.

A dear friend, Lady Caroline, suddenly appeared by her side, a mischievous glint in her eyes. "Ah, my dear Genevieve," she whispered, her gaze following Genevieve's to the enigmatic figure. "I see you've noticed our resident mystery."

Lady Caroline then took Genevieve by the arm and led her across the room towards the puzzle. As they approached

CHAPTER FIVE

him, he turned his gaze towards them. The room seemed to grow silent as their eyes met; he wore a black velvet mask, and his eyes were deep pools of brown that hinted at a profound depth and an unspoken history.

"Lady Sinclair," Lady Caroline introduced, "May I present the Marquess of Ravenswood."

Initially, he offered only a nod of acknowledgment. Then he took her hand and pressed his lips to it in a polite gesture that sent another wave of shivers down Genevieve's spine. His voice was low and resonant when he finally spoke. "Lady Sinclair," he said, holding her gaze with an intensity that left her momentarily breathless.

Their conversation began on an innocuous note, discussing the event and its attendees with polite interest. Yet as the evening progressed, their discussion delved into more profound topics – art, literature, philosophy – each word spoken revealing more layers to this intriguing man.

His intellect was evident in every sentence he uttered, and each question he posed left Genevieve thoughtful and intrigued. Yet it was his silence that intrigued her most—the moments when he would listen intently to her, his gaze unwavering, as if truly valuing her thoughts and opinions. It was a rare quality she found in the men of their society.

Despite his charm and charisma, a sense of mystery continued to shroud him. Every so often, he would lapse into silence, his gaze distant as if he were miles away. These moments piqued Genevieve's curiosity further. There was a melancholy about him, a silent struggle that resonated within her. It reminded her of the times she had felt the constraints of their society and yearned for something more.

Yet whenever she tried to delve deeper, he skillfully steered the conversation elsewhere. His rumored past remained just that - a mystery. A series of whispered tales of scandal and intrigue that had made him an enigma among their peers.

As the night drew to a close, they shared one final dance. His hand was warm against hers; his touch sent electric sparks through her body. The music played around them, but all Genevieve could hear was the rhythm of her heart pounding in her ears.

The dance ended all too soon, leaving Genevieve feeling both intrigued and puzzled by this enigmatic nobleman. As he escorted her back to her mother, she felt an inexplicable sense of disappointment at their parting.

The Marquess of Ravenswood bowed low before her once more before retreating into the crowd. As she watched him disappear among the masked figures, Genevieve couldn't help but wonder about this man who had captured her interest so thoroughly.

CHAPTER FIVE

Her heart fluttered in her chest as she contemplated the mysterious Marquess. Despite his rumored scandalous past and his brooding demeanor, she found herself irresistibly drawn towards him.

Lady Margaret urged her daughter once more, "Genevieve, darling, you must circulate and meet other guests. This evening presents such wonderful opportunities."

Genevieve nodded obediently, though her heart sank at the thought of making small talk with yet another parade of eligible bachelors. She longed to seek out the quiet company of her dear friend, Miss Charlotte Winslow. But before she could make her escape, a flash of color caught her eye.

Approaching them with a confident stride was none other than Viscount Hartfield, his striking features partially obscured by an ornate mask of crimson and gold. A mischievous smile played upon his lips as he bowed deeply before them.

"Lady Sinclair, you are a vision this evening—and your white feathered mask is divine," he proclaimed, his blue eyes sparkling with admiration. "Might I have the honor of this dance?"

Genevieve's pulse quickened as she placed her gloved hand in his outstretched palm. She could scarcely refuse, not when his very presence filled her with a giddy thrill that contrasted so sharply with the mundane dullness of the evening thus far.

As they swept onto the dance floor, Genevieve found herself momentarily lost in the cadence of the music and the warmth of Viscount Hartfield's embrace. His steps were assured his movements fluid as they glided amidst the swirling couples.

Yet her reverie was short-lived, for in the next breath, her gaze landed upon a sight that stirred an unexpected pang of jealousy within her breast. There, dancing with the effervescent Miss Charlotte, was the imposing figure of the Marquess of Ravenswood.

Genevieve's brow furrowed as she watched them, unable to tear her eyes away. The Marquess moved with an effortless grace, his broad shoulders cutting an elegant line as he guided Miss Charlotte through the intricate steps. A slight smile tugged at the corners of his mouth, betraying a hint of genuine amusement in her friend's lively conversation.

A fleeting twinge of envy gnawed at Genevieve's composure. She could not fathom why the sight should perturb her so. After all, the Marquess was but a recent acquaintance, a man she scarcely knew beyond the barest of introductions and the whispers that trailed his name.

And yet, there was an undeniable magnetism about him, a quiet intensity that called to her like a siren's song. She found herself inexplicably drawn to unravel the mysteries that seemed to cloak him like a shadowy mantle.

"Lady Sinclair?" Viscount Hartfield's voice cut through her distracted musings. "You seem preoccupied this evening."

Genevieve blinked, her cheeks flushing as she realized her gaze had lingered too long upon the Marquess and Miss Charlotte. "Forgive me, my lord," she murmured, forcing her attention back to her dance partner. "My mind has wandered, it seems."

A knowing gleam flickered in Viscount Hartfield's eyes as if he could sense the source of her distraction. But he merely offered her a roguish smile and pulled her a little closer as the music swelled around them.

"Then allow me to give you something far more engaging to ponder," he murmured, his breath warm against her ear as they swept across the floor.

Genevieve felt her pulse quicken once more, her earlier disquiet momentarily forgotten. The Viscount had a peculiar talent for commanding her focus, and his charm and wit were potent antidotes to the boredom that so often plagued her in these social spheres.

And yet, despite the pleasant diversion he provided, Genevieve could not entirely banish the lingering curiosity that had taken root within her regarding the enigmatic Marquess. As the dance drew to a close, she found her gaze straying once more, seeking out that imposing dark-clad figure amidst the swirling masks and gowns.

Six

The next day dawned grey and dreary, heavy raindrops pelting against the windows of Genevieve's family mansion. She sat by the drawing-room fire, her embroidery forgotten in her lap as her thoughts drifted back to the masquerade ball the previous evening. The Marquess of Ravenswood's intense gaze seemed forever etched into her memory; his brooding mystique was both intriguing and unsettling.

A sharp rap on the door roused Genevieve from her reverie. "Come in," she called, hastily smoothing her skirts as the door opened to reveal the familiar figure of Viscount Hartfield. A welcoming smile curved her lips, though it faltered slightly as she noticed the tightness around his eyes.

"Lady Sinclair," he greeted with a curt nod, striding into the room. "I had hoped we might continue our discussion from yesterday on the merits of Wordsworth's poetry."

"Of course, Viscount." Genevieve motioned for him to take a seat across from her. "I would be delighted to hear your thoughts on the matter."

Yet as he launched into an impassioned critique, Genevieve found her attention drifting, her mind inexplicably drawn back to the Marquess. She pictured his rugged features, the way his lips had curved into the faintest of smiles, when she challenged his brooding demeanor with a teasing remark.

"Lady Sinclair?" Viscount Hartfield's voice cut through her musings, laced with a sudden edge. "Am I boring you with my discourse?"

Genevieve blinked, heat rising to her cheeks. "Not at all, Viscount. Please, continue."

His jaw tightened fractionally. "I cannot help but sense your mind is elsewhere this morning." He leaned forward, blue eyes intent upon her face. "Might I enquire as to where your thoughts have wandered?"

An uncomfortable tingling ran down Genevieve's spine at the undercurrent of tension in his tone. "I...forgive me, Viscount. I am merely a bit tired from the festivities last night."

CHAPTER SIX

Viscount Hartfield's nostrils flared slightly. "I see. And was there perhaps someone at this event who captured your interest more than my philosophical musings?"

The abrupt shift in his demeanor took Genevieve by surprise. Gone was the effortless charm she had so admired, replaced by an almost predatory intensity that set her on edge. This was a side of the Viscount she had never witnessed before – a raw, possessive streak that both unnerved and intrigued her.

"Viscount, I did not mean to offend you," she began carefully. "You are a dear friend, and I value our discussions immensely. But I will not be claimed or possessed by any man, no matter his station." She lifted her chin, holding his gaze steadily. "I am my own mistress."

For a long moment, Viscount Hartfield stared at her, the muscle in his jaw twitching. Then, abruptly, he rose to his feet. "Forgive me, my lady. I have overstepped." He inclined his head stiffly. "I shall take my leave."

Genevieve watched him stride from the room, her hands trembling ever so slightly in the aftermath of his jealous outburst. She had always prided herself on being a keen judge of character, and yet the Viscount had revealed a side of himself she could scarcely have fathomed. As the rain lashed against the windows, she found her thoughts drifting inexorably back to the Marquess of Ravenswood and the secrets that seemed to lurk behind his smoldering gaze.

THE FOLLOWING DAY, Genevieve finds herself at another society event, this time a lavish garden party hosted by the Duchess of Norwood. Despite her reservations after her tense encounter with Viscount Hartfield, she attends, her curiosity piqued at the prospect of potentially encountering the enigmatic Marquess of Ravenswood once again.

As she mingles among the guests, sipping lemonade and making polite conversation, Genevieve catches sight of a tall, imposing figure across the perfectly manicured lawn. He was a specimen to look at without the black mask covering his eyes—it was hard for her to look away. His magnetism was quite appealing. Looking every inch the brooding aristocrat in his impeccably tailored jacket and cravat. Their eyes meet briefly, and Genevieve feels a delicious shiver run down her spine at the intensity of his stare.

Before she can overthink her actions, she excuses herself from her current company and begins weaving her way through the crowd towards the Marquess. Following a magnetic pull, she is determined to unravel the mystery surrounding this dark, compelling man – even if it means risking the raised eyebrows and wagging tongues of the *ton*.

Approaching the Marquess, Genevieve summons every ounce of her wit and bravado, refusing to be cowed by his imposing presence or the rumors that swirl around him like a thick fog.

"Marquess," she greets boldly, lifting her chin to meet his smoldering gaze. "What a delight to see you again so soon. I had feared our paths might not cross with such felicitous regularity."

A ghost of a smile tugs at the corner of his sculptured mouth, and Genevieve feels an answering spark of excitement in her belly. Up close, she can see the faint lines at the corners of his eyes, suggesting a life not quite as troubled as the gossipmongers would have one believe.

"Lady Sinclair," he rumbles, inclining his head ever so slightly. "I confess, I am surprised to find you seeking me out amidst such...polite company." His eyes glitter with a hint of challenge. "One might accuse you of harboring a rebellious streak, mingling with one of such disrepute as myself."

Genevieve arches one finely shaped brow, undaunted. "And if I do possess such a streak, sir? Might that not make our acquaintance all the more...intriguing?"

The Marquess regarded her appraisingly for a long moment before sweeping her a courtly bow. "In that case, my lady, I should be delighted to indulge your curiosity—should you dare to take the risk."

In the bright afternoon light, Genevieve studied the Marquess of Ravenswood anew, her gaze roving over the strong lines of his face and form. Unencumbered by the shadows and mystery of the masquerade, she could fully appreciate his striking features—the sharp angles of his jaw, the straight nose, the sensual curve of his lips. *Those lips,* she noted with a flutter in her belly, were curved in a slight, knowing smile as he returned her frank appraisal.

"You seem intrigued, my lady," he murmured, his deep voice a rich caress against her senses. Might I inquire as to the nature of your interest?"

Genevieve felt her cheeks warm ever so slightly at being so brazenly observed, but she refused to look away, meeting his gaze with an arch of her delicately shaped brows.

"One cannot help but admire a finely crafted work of art when presented with such," she parried, allowing a hint of challenge to lace her tone. "Surely you would not deny me the opportunity to appreciate true masculine beauty when I encounter it?"

A low chuckle rumbled from the Marquess's broad chest, his dark eyes glinting with an unmistakable masculine appreciation of his own. "I would be remiss to deny a lady of such discernment her…observations."

He leaned in ever so slightly, the rich, sandalwood scent of his cologne enveloping Genevieve's senses as he spoke in a low, conspiratorial tone.

"Though I must caution you, Lady Sinclair—to indulge oneself in such…admiration…often leads to a certain loss of propriety." His gaze dropped meaningfully to her lips before lifting once more, blazing with heated promise. "Are you prepared to risk such scandal?"

A delicious shiver traced its way down Genevieve's spine at the unmistakable undercurrent of flirtation in the Marquess's words. Here was a man unafraid to push the boundaries of decorum, to toy with the very rules that governed their stratified world. The idea was as terrifying as it was thrillingly seductive.

Lifting her chin in silent defiance of the voice of caution whispering at the back of her mind, she met his heated stare with a look of challenge.

"I am no wilting flower to be cowed by the threat of scandal, sir," she murmured, unable to resist the lure of his dangerous charisma. "Lead on…if you dare."

For an endless moment, the weight of the Marquess's regard seemed to pin Genevieve in place, the heated promise in his eyes sending her pulse fluttering like a trapped bird. Then, slowly, he inclined his head in grave acceptance of her daring rejoinder.

"As you wish, my lady," he rumbled, the low timbre of his voice sending tremors of anticipation ricocheting through her slender frame. "Let the scandal commence."

Just as the delicious tension between Genevieve and the Marquess seemed to reach a precipice, a familiar figure appeared at her elbow, shattering the heated moment like a bolt of lightning rending the sky.

"I see you've met my heathen of a nephew," the Duchess of Norwood remarked, fanning herself with fierce vigor.

"Aunt," the Marquess quipped, "Do not scare the lady off."

The Duchess hitched at his remark and glared at the man coming up behind the Marquess about to intrude on their fun. "Viscount Hartfield, how nice to—"

"Lady Sinclair," Viscount Hartfield's clipped tones cut through the charged air like a knife as he interrupted the Duchess. "I must insist you accompany me."

Without awaiting her response, he grasped her firmly by the elbow and began steering her away from the Marquess and the Duchess of Norwood—the muscles in his jaw ticking with obvious irritation.

Torn from the delightful frisson of attraction, Genevieve blinked in surprise and opened her mouth to protest, but

CHAPTER SIX

the Viscount allowed her no quarter. He swiftly guided her through the crowds of partygoers until they reached a secluded corner near the ornamental hedgerows, his grip on her arm unyielding.

Only when they were pretty alone did he release her, whirling to face her with smoldering eyes. "What in God's name do you think you're doing, cavorting so openly with that—that reprobate?"

Genevieve's eyes flashed with anger, her lips pursing in a moue of displeasure. "I beg your pardon, Viscount, but I was under no obligation to avoid the Marquess's company. He is a guest here, same as you and I."

Hartfield scoffed, raking an agitated hand through his brown locks. "Do not play the innocent with me, Lady Sinclair. That man is a scoundrel of the highest order—his very presence taints the air we breathe. For you to be seen conversing with him in such a...*familiar* manner..." He trailed off, nostrils flaring with barely restrained ire.

Squaring her delicate shoulders, Genevieve met his heated gaze with a look of calm defiance. "You seem to have forgotten yourself, sir. I am not your wife nor your betrothed—you have no claim over my actions or the company I choose to keep."

A muscle ticked in Hartfield's chiseled jaw, his blue eyes darkening to molten gold as he glowered down at her rebellious form. "You would do well to remember your place, my lady. A woman of your standing cannot afford to court scandal and ruin. Not if you wish to make a respectable match."

"Is that what concerns you?" she challenged, arching one finely shaped brow. "That I might be an insufficient prize for you to win?"

Her words seemed to strike a nerve, and the Viscount's expression contorted with a potent mix of desire and fury. Before Genevieve could draw another breath, he had seized her by the arm once more and was propelling her through a small gate in the hedgerow, away from prying eyes.

She opened her mouth to protest, but the words died on her lips as Hartfield abruptly pulled her flush against his robust frame and claimed her lips in a searing, possessive kiss.

Genevieve's world tilted on its axis as the Viscount's mouth moved hotly over hers, his tongue sweeping past her parted lips to taste her with bold, undeniable hunger. A whimper escaped her throat as the delicate muscles of his chest and shoulders flexed against her, pinning her in place as surely as iron shackles.

This was not the chaste brush of lips expected between a gentleman and a lady—this was raw, primal need given free rein. And good lord, despite the wrongness of it all,

Genevieve found herself powerless to resist the blazing temptation of the Viscount's ardent assault.

Her fingers curled into the delicate fabric of his jacket as a deep, liquid heat unfurled low in her belly, licking outward in molten waves with each skilled caress of his sinful mouth. When, at last, he broke the kiss, leaving them both gasping for air, Genevieve could only gaze up at him with dazed, heavy-lidded eyes, her lips still tingling from the brand of his passion.

"There," Hartfield rasped, his voice rough with the same desire that had her insides quivering like a plucked harp string. "Now the whole world shall know to whom you belong."

With those heated words still ringing in her ears, he released her and turned on his heel, disappearing back through the hedgerow and leaving Genevieve to sag weakly against the verdant foliage.

As she lifted a trembling hand to her lips, all thoughts of the enigmatic Marquess had fled, eclipsed by the blazing, terrifying reality of her reckoning with Viscount Hartfield's scorching, scandalous passion.

Seven

The rain pattered incessantly against the windowpanes, a constant reminder of the dreary day that had occurred in London. Genevieve sat in her parlor, gazing out at the gloomy sky with a wistful expression. The events of the previous evening, particularly her encounter with the enigmatic Marquess of Ravenswood and then the sudden assault of the Viscount, still lingered in her thoughts, causing a mixture of confusion and intrigue.

As she pondered her conundrum, a gentle knock at the door stirred her from her reverie. "Come in," she called out, her voice tinged with curiosity.

The door opened to reveal Miss Charlotte Winslow, Genevieve's dear friend, who had managed to arrive just before the heavens had opened up. Charlotte's cheeks were flushed from the brisk walk, and her eyes sparkled with the anticipation of sharing the latest gossip.

"Vivie, my dear!" Charlotte exclaimed, rushing forward to embrace her friend. "I am so glad I made it here before the rain truly began. It looks positively dreadful outside."

Genevieve returned the embrace, a genuine smile gracing her lips. "Charlotte, it is always a pleasure to see you. I must admit, I am rather relieved to have some company on this dreary day."

The two young ladies settled themselves on the plush sofa, the warmth of the crackling fire chasing away the chill that had seeped into the room. *Carrot*, Genevieve's faithful calico cat, leaped onto her lap, curling up contentedly as she gently stroked his soft fur.

"I heard whispers of your dance with Lord Huntley," Charlotte began, her eyes alight with mischief. "They say he was quite taken with you, my dear."

Carrot lay curled up contentedly on the chaise lounge, oblivious to the storm raging outside. "What news?" Genevieve asked, trying to detour the gossip away from her, knowing full well that Miss Charlotte Winslow was full of the latest tattle.

"Have you heard the latest gossip about the Marquess of Ravenswood?" Charlotte leaned forward conspiratorially, her eyes alight with the thrill of sharing a juicy tidbit. "Rumor has it that he was involved in a duel some years ago, and his opponent did not survive the encounter!"

Genevieve's breath caught in her throat as a chill ran down her spine. The brooding nobleman had indeed captivated her with his mysterious allure, but the suggestion of such a dark and violent past gave her pause.

"Good heavens, Charlotte! Surely you cannot be serious," she exclaimed, her brow furrowing with concern. "A duel is a grave matter and one that could lead to ruination if the truth were to come to light."

Charlotte nodded eagerly, reveling in the scandalous details. "That's not all, my dear. There are whispers that the duel was fought over a woman—a woman whose identity has been carefully guarded all these years. Some say she was the Marquess's mistress, while others claim she was promised to another man entirely."

Genevieve felt her stomach twist into knots. The Marquess's alluring mystique had drawn her in like a moth to a flame, but now the shadows of his rumored past cast a pall over her growing fascination. Could a man capable of such violence and deceit ever be worthy of her affections?

"I want nothing more to do with him," Genevieve declared, her voice trembling ever so slightly. "A man with such a tarnished reputation and disregard for propriety is not someone I wish to associate with, no matter how captivating he may appear on the surface."

Charlotte's expression turned sly, her curiosity piqued by Genevieve's vehement reaction. "And what of the dashing Viscount Hartfield? Surely, *his* charms have not escaped your notice."

A flush crept into Genevieve's cheeks as she recalled the stolen moments she had shared with the charming nobleman. His easy wit and genuine interest in her thoughts and desires had been a breath of fresh air amidst the stifling expectations of society.

"The Viscount has been most attentive," she admitted, unable to suppress a shy smile. "In fact, he has even…" Genevieve paused, considering whether to divulge such an intimate detail.

Charlotte leaned forward eagerly, her eyes wide with anticipation. "Go on, Vivie! You must tell me!"

Taking a deep breath, Genevieve confided in her closest friend. "The Viscount has kissed me, Charlotte. It was a moment of pure bliss, one that made me feel truly alive and understood for the first time in my life."

Charlotte's eyes grew wide as saucers, her gloved hands flying to her mouth in a bid to stifle the delighted squeal that escaped her lips. "Oh, Vivie! You sly little minx! You must tell me everything about this kiss with the dashing Viscount Hartfield!"

Genevieve felt heat bloom in her cheeks, her gaze dropping demurely as she recalled the heady rush of that stolen moment. "It was utterly divine, Charlotte. A mere brush of his lips against mine, and yet I felt as though the world around us had ceased to exist."

"How terribly romantic!" Charlotte gushed, leaning forward eagerly. "Where did this amorous encounter take place? In the gardens, perhaps? Or maybe a secluded alcove during one of the grand balls?"

Genevieve's lips wistfully smacked as she recounted the details: "It was at the Norwood garden party, of all places. We had been engaged in a lively discussion about poetry when suddenly," Genevieve lied, "Our eyes met, and the air seemed to crackle with an undeniable spark."

Charlotte swooned, fanning herself dramatically. "And then? Oh, do not leave me in suspense, my dear!"

"His gaze fell to my lips, and before I could draw breath, he had pulled me into his embrace," Genevieve continued, her voice dropping to a hushed whisper. "Our lips met, and at that moment, I felt as though I had finally found the grand passion I had always dreamed of."

"How utterly scandalous!" Charlotte exclaimed, her eyes shining with delight. "And what of propriety? Surely you did not allow the Viscount to take too many liberties?"

Genevieve lifted her chin, a hint of defiance flashing in her azure eyes. "I am a woman of virtue, Charlotte, but I will not deny the stirrings of my heart. The Viscount's kiss was a fleeting moment of pure bliss, one that I shall forever cherish."

Charlotte's expression softened, and she reached out to give Genevieve's hand a gentle squeeze. "I am overjoyed for you, my friend. Truly, you deserve to find the kind of love that sets your soul afire."

A playful grin tugged at the corners of Charlotte's lips. "Speaking of love and courtship, I have news of my own to share."

Genevieve's brow arched inquisitively. "Oh? Do tell, dear Charlotte!"

"Lord Rhodes has asked for my hand in marriage, and I have accepted!" Charlotte beamed, her cheeks flushed with happiness.

A squeal of delight escaped Genevieve's lips, and she threw her arms around her friend in a warm embrace. "Charlotte, that is wonderful news! Lord Rhodes is a fine gentleman, and I cannot think of a more perfect match."

CHAPTER SEVEN

The two friends clung to each other, their joyous laughter mingling with the pitter-patter of raindrops against the windowpanes. At that moment, the weight of societal expectations and the whispers of scandal seemed to fade away, replaced by the pure, unbridled happiness of two young hearts daring to dream of love and all its possibilities.

Eight

The rain had stopped momentarily, granting a brief respite from the unrelenting downpour that had kept Genevieve confined within the walls of her family's townhouse for days. As the carriage rolled to a stop before the imposing façade of Lord Westborough's grand mansion, Genevieve felt a flutter of anticipation mingled with trepidation.

This was to be the last ball of the London Season, a final opportunity for the city's elite to mingle and forge alliances before retreating to their country estates. For those already paired, it was a chance to revel in newfound attachments, while for the unmatched, it represented a dwindling hope of securing a suitable match.

Lady Margaret Sinclair's expression was etched with concern as she alighted from the carriage, her gaze sweeping over the crowds of guests already assembled. "Vivie, my dear," she murmured, her tone laced with a mother's desperation. "This may be your final chance to make an impression."

Genevieve offered a tight smile, her heart heavy with the weight of her mother's expectations. Though she understood the societal pressures that bound them, her longing for a love that transcended mere convenience or fortune had only grown stronger with each passing day.

As they entered the grand ballroom, Genevieve's senses were immediately assailed by the sights and sounds that had become so familiar – the glittering chandeliers, the hum of polite conversation, the strains of the orchestra tuning their instruments. Yet, her mind kept drifting to the memory of the Viscount's lips upon hers, the unexpected kiss that had left her breathless and confused. *Could a proposal be next?*

Determined to maintain her composure, Genevieve accepted the hand of the first bachelor who requested her for a dance. As they joined the whirl of coupled figures, she could not help but notice the radiant smiles and knowing glances exchanged between those who had already secured their future partnerships.

Lady Margaret's gaze followed her daughter's every step, her brow furrowed with concern. Genevieve knew her mother's fears all too well – the prospect of her remaining unmatched, a burden to her family, and a source of endless gossip.

As the dance progressed, Genevieve found herself distracted, her thoughts pulled in a dozen different directions. The Viscount's handsome features kept materializing before her, only to be replaced by the brooding countenance of the Marquess of Ravenswood, his piercing gaze seeming to bore into her very soul.

So engrossed was she in her inner turmoil that she failed to notice the approach of another dancer until it was too late. With a startled gasp, Genevieve collided with a solid form, the force of the impact nearly sending her stumbling.

"Forgive me, my lady," a deep, familiar voice rumbled, steadying hands gripping her arms to prevent her fall.

Genevieve's breath caught in her throat as her gaze met the intense stare of the Marquess himself. His brown eyes seemed to scorch her very being, igniting a flame deep within her that she dared not contemplate.

"Lord Ravenswood," she managed, her voice emerging as little more than a breathless whisper. "I... I did not see you there."

A ghost of a smile played across the Marquess's lips, his touch lingering a moment longer than propriety dictated. "Clearly," he murmured, his tone laced with a hint of amusement. "Perhaps you would do me the honor of the next dance? It would seem we are in dire need of a buffer between us and the rest of the room."

Genevieve's cheeks flushed with a mixture of embarrassment and something far more dangerous – a spark of undeniable attraction that threatened to consume her from within.

The grand ballroom was a whirlwind of colors and movement, the air filled with the sound of laughter and the strains of the string quartet. Genevieve felt as if she were caught in a dream, her senses overwhelmed by the luxury that surrounded her. As she gracefully navigated the dance floor, her gown swirling with each step, she found herself face-to-face with the one man who seemed to haunt her every waking thought.

His piercing gaze held hers, and for a moment, the rest of the world faded away. "My dear Lady Sinclair," he murmured, his voice a low, velvet caress that sent a shiver down her spine. "Might I request the honor of a private audience?"

Genevieve's breath caught in her throat, her pulse quickening at the mere thought of being alone with this enigmatic man. Yet, even as a part of her yearned to indulge in the forbidden, she knew she must maintain her propriety. "I'm afraid I must decline, my lord," she replied, her tone calm and measured, betraying none of the turmoil that raged within her.

CHAPTER EIGHT

The Marquess inclined his head, a ghost of a smile playing upon his lips. "As you wish, my lady." With a fluid motion, he melted back into the crowd, leaving Genevieve to wonder if their encounter had been mere fancy.

Before she could collect her thoughts, a familiar voice broke through the haze. "Lady Genevieve, my darling, there you are." Viscount Hartfield appeared at her side, his blue eyes sparkling with warmth and affection.

Genevieve felt her heart lurch, the memory of his kiss still fresh in her mind. The gentle press of his lips against hers, the way his fingers had tangled in her hair, the scent of his cologne enveloping her senses – it had all been so intoxicating, yet so utterly confusing.

"Viscount," she breathed, struggling to regain her composure. "I did not expect to see you here."

"And miss the chance to gaze upon your radiant beauty?" he teased, his smile disarming. "Perish the thought, my dear."

As he swept her into a dance, Genevieve found herself lost in the moment, her body moving in perfect synchronicity with his. Yet, even as she reveled in his presence, a part of her longed for the mystery and intensity that surrounded the Marquess.

The Marquess was like a siren's call, luring her toward the unknown with promises of passion and adventure. His very existence seemed to challenge the rigid confines of society, igniting a fire within her that she had long thought extinguished. *Duel be damned!*

And yet, the Viscount offered a different kind of comfort, a familiarity that soothed her soul. His love was a steady flame, burning bright and true, a beacon in the darkness that threatened to consume her.

As the music swelled around them, Genevieve found herself torn between two worlds, two men who held her heart captive in ways she could scarcely comprehend. The Marquess was the embodiment of her deepest desires, a temptation she could barely resist. But the Viscount represented the life she had been groomed for, a life of security and propriety.

At that moment, as she danced in the arms of the Viscount, Genevieve knew she stood at a crossroads. The path she chose would shape her destiny, for better or for worse. And as the night wore on, the weight of her decision grew heavier with each passing moment.

Genevieve's heart raced as she excused herself from the Viscount's presence, her feet carrying her swiftly across the ballroom and out onto the terrace. The cool night air caressed her flushed cheeks, offering little relief from the storm of emotions that swirled within her.

CHAPTER EIGHT

Ducking behind a marble column, she pressed her back against the cool stone, her fingers clutching at the delicate fabric of her gown. *Was this what love felt like – this dizzying maelstrom of desire and doubt, of longing and fear?* Her chest rose and fell with each ragged breath as she struggled to make sense of the conflicting feelings that threatened to overwhelm her.

The Viscount was the epitome of everything she had been taught to desire – a perfect gentleman, wealthy and well-respected, his love for her a steady flame that promised security and comfort. And yet, the mere thought of his steadfast caress, his tender kisses, no longer set her heart ablaze with passion. Instead, her treacherous mind conjured the image of the Marquess, his smoldering gaze piercing her very soul, igniting a fire within her that burned with a fierce intensity she could scarcely comprehend.

Lifting her gaze to the twinkling stars above, Genevieve felt as though she could scarcely breathe, the weight of her indecision pressing down upon her like a physical force. She stepped over to the railing, her eyes drawn to the shadowed gardens below, where the Marquess strolled arm-in-arm with a young debutante, their laughter carried on the evening breeze.

A sharp pang of envy lanced through Genevieve's heart as she watched the pair, her fingers tightening their grip on the cool stone railing. How easy it must be for the

Marquess to cast aside the constraints of society and indulge in his every whim, consequences be damned. And yet, even as she envied his freedom, a part of her longed to be the one at his side, to bask in the warmth of his approval, to lose herself in the depths of his passion.

The Viscount was the safe choice, the path laid out before her by virtue of her birth and station. But the Marquess... he represented the unknown, a tantalizing glimpse of a world where love burned bright and fierce, untamed by the shackles of propriety and expectation.

As she watched the Marquess and his companion disappear into the shadows of the garden, Genevieve felt a single, traitorous tear slip down her cheek. She brushed it away with trembling fingers, her heart torn asunder by the warring desires that threatened to consume her.

At that moment, she knew she truly stood at a crossroads, her future hanging in the balance. Would she surrender to the safe embrace of the Viscount, sacrificing her own desires for the sake of duty and propriety? Or would she heed the siren call of the Marquess, plunging headfirst into a world of passion and scandal, consequences be damned?

The decision was hers and hers alone. As the night wore on, the weight of that choice grew heavier with each passing moment, pressing down upon her until she felt as though she might suffocate beneath its crushing weight.

Nine

Genevieve was left in the tumultuous swirl of a grand ballroom that suddenly felt much too confining. An odd twinge of regret prickled at her conscience, a feeling as unexpected as the raindrops that had descended upon London just hours prior.

Drawn by an inexplicable urge for solitude, Genevieve found herself navigating through the mansion's labyrinthine hallways. The opulent chandeliers and gold-trimmed tapestries fell away as she made her escape from the stifling chatter and scrutinizing glances of the elite.

She found herself in the sanctuary of the moonlit garden down below, its serene tranquility offering a stark contrast to the lively cacophony she had left behind. Her silken gown rustled softly against the dew-kissed grass as she moved amongst rose bushes laden with crimson blooms, their thorny branches reaching out like silent confidants, ready to hear her secrets.

As she paused under the soft glow of the moonlight, a cool evening breeze danced around her, teasing loose strands of her hair and whispering secrets in her ear. Genevieve took a deep breath, inhaling the heady fragrance of roses mingling with the crisp night air. A yearning stirred within her heart, a longing for something more profound than what her world offered - a connection that transcended societal expectations and went beyond class boundaries.

She leaned against a marble bench, its calm surface grounding her amidst the storm of uncertainty brewing within her. The stars twinkled above like distant witnesses to her turmoil, their soft glow reflected in her sapphire eyes. "Why must the heart be drawn to what we are told to avoid?" she whispered into the velvety darkness.

Her words hung in the air, suspended like dewdrops on the petal of a rose. It was a quiet admission of her inner conflict, a question posed to the night sky and the silent roses surrounding her. And though the night offered no answers, it held her words with a comforting embrace, wrapping them in its tranquil cloak as Genevieve sought solace under the moonlit sky.

Her contemplative silence was disrupted by a voice that caused her to stiffen slightly. It was a familiar, low, melodic tone that had the power to draw her attention even in the most crowded of ballrooms. She turned slowly to see the Viscount emerging from the shadows of the garden. The gentle light from the scattered lanterns painted a softer hue on his striking features, his dark brown hair glinting with hints of auburn.

He sauntered toward her with an effortless grace that was so inherently his, his blue eyes reflecting the dim lantern light. "Escaping the stifling conformity of the ballroom, Lady Sinclair?" he queried, an amused smile tugging at his lips.

"I find the company of roses far more genuine," she retorted lightly, her heart beating an uneasy rhythm against her ribcage.

He laughed, a rich sound that seemed to meld with the evening air. "A fair point indeed," he agreed. "These roses pale in comparison to your radiance."

His words hung in the air between them, and Genevieve forced a smile onto her face, aware of his intent gaze on her. She tucked a stray curl behind her ear, trying to keep her emotions under wraps.

"May I accompany you on this stroll?" Alexander asked formally, extending his arm in invitation.

Genevieve hesitated for a moment before placing her hand lightly on his arm. As they strolled together along the winding path, their surroundings were bathed in a spectral glow that lent an otherworldly charm to their meeting.

In an attempt to dispel the undercurrent of tension, Alexander began speaking about their shared love for art. He recited a sonnet from memory, his voice dipping and rising in perfect cadence with the verses. It was a poignant piece that spoke of unrequited love and longing - emotions that seemed to mirror the turmoil in Genevieve's heart.

Genevieve found herself drawn into the conversation, her responses sharp and thoughtful. Yet, as they delved deeper into their discourse, she felt a gnawing uncertainty. Her mind was a battlefield of conflicting desires - the comfort of Alexander's familiarity against the intrigue of the Marquess's enigma, societal duty against heart's longing. The undercurrent of her thoughts was a tumultuous sea threatening to pull her under.

And so they walked on, two figures bathed in moonlight, their words painting the silence with hues of shared interests and subtle flirtations. But beneath it all, Genevieve felt the pull of an unseen tide - one that threatened to upend her carefully constructed world.

As they strolled through the garden, Genevieve could sense the shift in the Viscount's demeanor. His words, laden with admiration and affection, seemed to dance around a question he dared not ask. She knew, with a certainty that both thrilled and terrified her, that he wanted to kiss her again. The memory of their previous encounter, the gentle pressure of his lips against hers, sent a shiver down her spine.

But this time, Genevieve held back. She turned her face slightly, letting his words wash over her like a gentle breeze but not allowing them to take root. It was not that she didn't enjoy his company or appreciate his attention. In fact, she found herself entirely drawn to his wit and charm. But there was a part of her, a persistent whisper in the back of her mind, that questioned whether this was indeed what she wanted.

As they walked, Genevieve's thoughts drifted to the Marquess of Ravenswood. His brooding intensity and air of mystery had captured her interest from the moment they met. There was something about him, a depth that she longed to explore, that made her feel alive in a way she had never experienced before. And yet, society's whispers about his scandalous past gave her pause. *Was she willing to risk her reputation, her very future, for a man she barely knew?*

Genevieve's heart felt torn in two, pulled in opposite directions by the Viscount's familiarity and the Marquess's allure. She knew that she would eventually have to make a choice, but the thought filled her with trepidation. *How could she decide between two men who, in their ways, made her feel things she had never felt before?*

Ten

Under the moon's silken glow, Genevieve allowed herself to drink in the Viscount's eloquence and the enthusiasm of his poetic recitations. Each verse he shared seemed a veiled confession of the attraction simmering between them, yet she couldn't help but feel a sense of cautious resistance. Knowing his reputation and the societal ramifications of her every interaction, she weighed her responses with care, her wit as much a party as it was an engagement.

As they strolled along the garden path, Viscount Hartfield's voice wove a tapestry of words, each one carefully chosen to captivate his audience. "In the depths of your eyes, I find myself lost, a wanderer in search of a home I never knew I sought," he murmured, his gaze fixed upon Genevieve's face.

She felt the weight of his words, the intensity of his stare, and a part of her longed to surrender to the enchantment he so effortlessly spun. Yet, a voice within her whispered caution, reminding her of the expectations that bound her and the consequences of straying too far from the path laid out before her. His proposal was nearing; she knew so in her heart.

Their promenade led them beside a serene fountain, its gentle cascade providing a soothing backdrop to their conversation. Genevieve seized a moment of calm to reflect, her heart pulsing not just with the thrill of the Viscount's proximity but with the haunting memory of the Marquess's stoic demeanor as he withdrew into the throng.

The moonlight danced across the Viscount's chiseled features as he leaned closer, his voice dropping to an intimate murmur. *"She walks in beauty, like the night / Of cloudless climes and starry skies,"* he recited, the words of Lord Byron caressing the air between them.

Genevieve felt her breath catch in her throat, the poetry resonating deep within her soul. For a fleeting moment, she allowed herself to become lost in the cadence of the Viscount's rich timbre, his words painting a vivid tapestry that mirrored the ethereal beauty surrounding them.

"And all that's best of dark and bright / Meet in her aspect and her eyes," he continued, his gaze locked upon hers as if she were the very embodiment of the verse. A shiver coursed

through Genevieve's being, her defenses momentarily lowered by the sheer power of his recitation.

Genevieve's lips parted, a soft exhalation escaping them as she wrestled with the turmoil brewing in her heart. The Viscount's words had ensnared her senses, and she found herself enthralled by his charisma and the promise of passion that lingered beneath the surface of each carefully chosen phrase.

"My Lord, your command of the poet's craft is truly unparalleled," she managed, her voice a mere whisper in the stillness of the night. "Yet, I fear the beauty you describe pales in comparison to the artistry with which you wield such words."

Her reply was both a compliment and a subtle deflection, an attempt to regain her composure and maintain the propriety that society demanded. Yet, even as she spoke, a part of her longed to succumb to the intoxicating allure of the Viscount's seduction, to surrender to the tempestuous desires that threatened to consume her.

The poetic lines that he recited settled upon her like a mist—inspiring yet impossible to grasp—she wondered if his words were crafted to enamor or if they held a more profound truth. Was he sincere in his affections, or was she merely another conquest to be won and discarded?

As if sensing her inner turmoil, Viscount Hartfield reached out and gently took her hand in his. "Lady Sinclair, I cannot help but feel that fate has brought us together on this enchanting evening. Your beauty, your intellect, your very essence calls to me like a siren's song."

Genevieve felt the warmth of his touch, the sincerity in his voice, and for a moment, she allowed herself to imagine a future where she could follow her heart's desires. But the weight of duty and societal expectations quickly pulled her back to reality.

With a gentle smile, she withdrew her hand from his grasp. "Viscount Hartfield, your words are as charming as they are poetic."

A flicker of disappointment crossed Alexander's face, but he quickly masked it with a nod of understanding. "Of course, my Lady. Forgive me if I have overstepped. It is merely a testament to the depth of my admiration for you."

Genevieve felt a pang of regret at the necessity of her words, but she knew that to indulge in the Viscount's affections would be to invite a proposal she was not quite ready for.

A sense of duty propelled her to steer their conversation toward neutral topics gently, and Alexander, with the slightest flicker of disappointment, obliged. In the

CHAPTER TEN

exchange of pleasantries, Genevieve examined her inner turmoil, the societal expectations clashing with her genuine desires, creating an inner dissonance yearning for resolution.

The path wove back toward the mansion, the distant strains of a string quartet drifting through the night air. It was here that the unexpected occurred—a stirring in the nearby hedges. From the foliage stepped none other than the Marquess of Ravenswood himself, his countenance unreadable in the dim light. Yet, his eyes fixated upon Genevieve with an intensity that sent a charge through the air.

Genevieve froze, caught between the two suitors, as the gravity of the moment settled around them like a shroud. Alexander's demeanor shifted, a taut edge creeping into his normally unruffled façade. A silent battle of wills ensued, aristocratic restraint holding back an ocean of unsaid words.

The Marquess, with an apologetic glance toward Genevieve, explained his intrusion. "Forgive me; I was seeking a respite from the festivities and had not anticipated this rendezvous." Despite his explanation, the undercurrent of something more profound, some unspoken allegiance or challenge, passed between the men.

Lady Sinclair felt torn—as though she were the embodiment of the battleground on which these two men warily circled each other. Yet, it was her own heart's conflict, reflected in the eyes of the Marquess and the Viscount, that whispered of her power to either bridge their discord or allow it to divide. She knew she must navigate this triangle with astuteness and grace, for her decision carried the weight of her future—a tapestry woven from the threads of desire, reputation, and the unyielding customs of the time.

Raising her chin, Genevieve summoned the poise expected of a lady of her station. "Gentlemen, surely there is room enough in these gardens for all to enjoy the evening air." Her words sliced through the tension, a gentle reminder of decorum.

Alexander, ever the charmer, was the first to respond. "Of course, my Lady. You are quite right." He offered a curt nod to the Marquess, though his eyes betrayed a lingering challenge.

The Marquess inclined his head in return, his expression harboring a hint of amusement. "I would not dream of disrupting your evening stroll," he remarked, his gaze finding Genevieve's once more. "Though, if you would indulge me with but a moment of your time on the morrow, I should be most grateful."

Genevieve's breath caught in her throat, the weight of his request hanging in the air between them. Granting such a favor would be highly improper, yet she found herself captivated by the promise of unraveling the mysteries that seemed to enshroud this enigmatic nobleman endlessly. With a sidelong glance at Alexander, she replied, "Very well, my Lord. I shall endeavor to find a suitable opportunity."

Eleven

As the quartet's final notes fade into the background, Genevieve fixes her gaze upon the rival suitors before her. The sound of her own voice breaks the charged silence, steady and more assertive than she feels inside. "Gentlemen, though your company is most esteemed, I find the hour grows late, and I must retire." With a grace inherited from her noble upbringing, she offers a demure curtsy—a silent dismissal.

Her words hang in the air as both men, taken aback by her poise, offer their goodnights with equal parts of admiration and frustration. As Genevieve turns back to the house, her heart races with the thrill of her autonomy. The events of the evening have ignited within her an ember of resolve to take command of her future.

Genevieve's mind is tumultuous with thoughts of the Viscount's veiled pain and the Marquess' alluring charm. Yet, she resolves not to be swayed by whispers of scandal or the allure of poetry. With each step, she vows to discern the true character of these men, for she knows superficial gestures or societal expectations will not win her heart.

Genevieve's steps echoed through the dimly lit corridors as she hurried away, her mind a whirlwind of emotion. The encounter with the Viscount and the Marquess had left her reeling, torn between propriety and the stirrings of her heart. She knew she must seek solace, lest her composure crumble before the prying eyes of the ton.

Turning a corner, she spied her mother, Lady Margaret, engaged in idle conversation with a cluster of matrons. Genevieve swiftly approached, her voice steady despite the storm within. "Mama, I find myself quite fatigued. Might we depart?"

Lady Margaret's keen gaze immediately fixed upon her daughter's face, studying the taut lines around Genevieve's eyes and the uncharacteristic flush upon her cheeks. A silent understanding passed between them—a mother's intuition recognizing the turmoil her child sought to conceal. With a curt nod, Lady Margaret excused them both, offering no explanation to her stunned companions.

The carriage awaited them just beyond the manor's grand entrance, the soft patter of raindrops dancing upon its roof.

CHAPTER ELEVEN

Genevieve ascended first, settling onto the plush velvet seat as her mother joined her. The door closed with a resounding thud, wrapping them in silence save for the rhythmic clops of the horses' hooves.

Lady Margaret's eyes remained fixed upon the window, permitting her daughter the stillness to collect her thoughts. Only when they had traversed several blocks did she turn to Genevieve, her voice a whisper that belied a lifetime of experience. "Did the Viscount propose this evening?"

Genevieve's gaze fell to her trembling hands, her fingers tightly laced. "No, Mama. He did not." The words carried a weight far greater than their simplicity, for they spoke of dreams deferred and paths yet undefined.

GENEVIEVE ENTERS THE MANSION, her mind abuzz with newfound determination. She seeks the solitude of her chamber, eager to escape the stifling confines of the ballroom and the watchful eyes of the *ton*. As she walks, she reflects on the events of the evening, her thoughts a tangled web of emotions.

The Marquess's enigmatic presence continues to haunt her. His rumored past and the whispers of scandal that followed him like a shadow intrigue her, yet she cannot ignore the vulnerability she glimpsed in his eyes. She yearns to know the truth behind the facade, to unravel the secrets that shroud him like a cloak.

Yet, she is equally drawn to the Viscount's charm and intelligence. His poetic recitations and eloquent speeches have stirred something within her, a longing for a connection that transcends the superficialities of society. However, she cannot shake the feeling that beneath his polished exterior lies a web of secrets and complexities that she has yet to understand fully.

As Genevieve reaches her chamber, she pauses at the threshold, her mind racing. She knows she cannot rush into a decision, for her heart and her future hang in the balance. She must proceed with caution, guided by her instincts and the wisdom of her own heart.

Genevieve's retreat to the solitude of her chambers is interrupted by a tentative knock at her door. Expecting a maid or perhaps her sister, she is surprised to find instead her dear friend Miss Charlotte standing in the hallway, a look of earnest concern upon her face.

"A moment of your time on my way home," Charlotte begins, her voice a mix of hesitance and urgency, "I could not help but observe ... the tension between you and the two gentlemen this evening."

Genevieve's heart skips a beat. She had not expected anyone to notice the silent battle in the garden. "Oh, it was nothing," she says, attempting to brush it off with a nonchalant wave of her hand. "It was just a misunderstanding."

But Charlotte is not convinced. "My dear Genevieve, I may not be the most perceptive person in the world, but even I could see the sparks flying between you and both Lord Hartfield and the Marquess."

Genevieve sighs, knowing that she cannot keep her turmoil hidden from her friend. "I cannot deny that I am... drawn to both of them in different ways," she admits. "But it is all so complicated."

Charlotte nods in understanding. "I know," she says. "Lord Hartfield is everything a society lady could want: charming, handsome, and wealthy. But the Marquess... there is something about him that is both alluring and dangerous."

Genevieve cannot help but agree. The Marquess is a man of mystery and contradictions. He is rumored to have a scandalous past, but there is also a vulnerability in his eyes that she cannot ignore.

"I do not know what to do," Genevieve says, her voice

laced with frustration. "My heart tells me one thing, but my head tells me another."

Charlotte takes her hand. "You must listen to your heart, my dear. It will never lead you astray."

Genevieve looks at her friend, her eyes filled with uncertainty. "But what if my heart leads me to ruin?"

"Then you will face it with your head held high," Charlotte says firmly. "You are a strong and intelligent woman, Vivie. You can overcome any obstacle that comes your way."

Genevieve takes a deep breath, feeling a renewed sense of resolve. "You are right," she says. "I will not let fear dictate my choices. I will follow my heart, no matter where it leads me."

Charlotte smiles. "That is the spirit," she says. "Now, let us get some rest. You have a big day ahead of you tomorrow."

With that, Charlotte bid Genevieve goodnight and left her alone with her thoughts. Genevieve stands by the window, looking out at the rain and Charlotte's carriage pulling away. She knows that the path ahead will not be easy, but she is determined to face it with courage and grace.

CHAPTER ELEVEN

THE NIGHT DESCENDED upon the estate like a velvet shroud, enveloping the world in its peaceful embrace. Yet for Genevieve, slumber eluded her, her mind a tempestuous sea of thoughts and desires. A crack of thunder shattered the stillness, its resonant rumble announcing the arrival of a summer storm. The dancing illumination of lightning filtered through the delicate lace curtains, casting fleeting shadows across her bedchamber.

Genevieve stirred beneath the covers, her satin nightgown clinging to the slender curves of her frame as she turned restlessly. Memories of the Viscount's stolen kiss flooded her senses, the ghost of his touch lingering upon her lips like the lingering caress of a phantom. In those heated moments, she had felt a fire ignite within her—a yearning for passion, for a love that transcended the rigid confines of propriety.

Yet now, in the sanctuary of her bed, doubt crept in like a noxious fog. Did she truly desire the Viscount's ardent embrace, or was it merely the thrill of the forbidden that had set her heart racing? With each flash of lightning, she envisioned the smoldering gaze of the Marquess, his enigmatic allure a siren call that threatened to drown her in its depths.

A heavy sigh escaped her parted lips as she turned her face toward the window, watching the rivulets of rain streak down the glass like tears shed by the heavens themselves.

The storm that raged outside mirrored the tempest within her soul, a maelstrom of conflicting emotions and desires that left her adrift in a sea of uncertainty.

Genevieve's thoughts drifted to the inescapable truth that her future was not entirely her own. As the daughter of a noble family, she was expected to make a match that would solidify her family's standing and secure their legacy. The notion of marrying a man she did not love weighed heavily upon her heart, a bitter pill to swallow for one who had always dreamed of a love that would set her soul ablaze.

Another peal of thunder rumbled through the night, its ominous echo a harbinger of the storm that brewed within her. Would she be forced to sacrifice her heart's desires upon the altar of societal expectations? Or would she find the courage to defy convention and forge her own path, no matter the consequences?

As the rain continued to rattle against the windowpane, Genevieve felt a solitary tear escape the corner of her eye, trailing a glistening path down her flushed cheek.

Twelve

Genevieve awoke to the pale wash of dawn spilling across her chamber, the light teasing the edges of her dreams and beckoning her back to the waking world. She lay for a moment, nestled among the linens, as fragments of the previous night's events wove through her thoughts—a tangled tapestry of glances and half-whispered words.

A letter perched upon her dressing table captured her attention, its presence as silent as conspicuous. The seal, a majestic raven embossed in dark wax, spoke of its sender before she even grazed the parchment with her fingertips. It was an emblem that set her pulse racing—the Marquess of Ravenswood had penned her a letter.

With hands that trembled ever so slightly, Genevieve broke the seal and unfolded the vellum. The script that met her eyes was fluid and assured, each stroke of ink a testament to the character of its author.

> *Lady Sinclair,*
>
> *Dare I invite you to attend the art gallery this afternoon? I'll be waiting with bated breath by the Turner.*
>
> *Yours,*
> *Ravenswood*

An invitation lay before her, couched in courteous terms but daring in its intent—a private viewing at one of London's most esteemed art galleries.

The room seemed to close in around Genevieve as she contemplated the proposal. To be seen in public with the Marquess, unchaperoned no less, would set tongues wagging with scandalous delight. Yet, how could she decline an offer that spoke so keenly to her interests? Art was a passion they shared—an intimate language that transcended the spoken word.

As the church bells chimed through the city, marking the passing hours, Genevieve's resolve solidified. She would attend. The decision was not made lightly; she understood well the precarious balance of reputation and desire. She chose a gown that whispered elegance rather than shouted

CHAPTER TWELVE

opulence—a dove-grey silk that complimented her eyes and spoke of quiet sophistication.

Her note to Lady Margaret was crafted with equal care, imploring understanding of her need to seek solace within the sanctuary of their family church. It was a small deception, but Genevieve felt it was necessary to protect not only herself but also those she held dear from any potential fallout.

The city streets teemed with life as Genevieve stepped out into the afternoon bustle. Carriages rolled past, their occupants ensconced within, while street vendors called out their wares with lyrical persistence. The gallery loomed ahead, its facade unassuming yet imposing—an island of tranquility amid London's relentless tide.

A footman waited at the entrance, his livery discreet and his nod one of recognition as Genevieve approached. He held open the door for her and murmured a greeting as she passed from daylight into the hushed interior where art and beauty reigned supreme.

Her heart danced with a rhythm against her ribs; each beat, an echo of anticipation mingled with fear. This meeting was no ordinary affair—it bore weight beyond measure in its promise and peril.

Genevieve took a steadying breath as she entered the gallery. The artworks adorning the walls were masterpieces

—each canvas and sculpture a silent sentinel to human creativity. And there he stood amidst them—the Marquess himself—his figure both part of this refined world and yet starkly apart from it.

Their eyes met across the expanse, a myriad of emotions conveyed in a single glance. The Marquess's gaze held hers with unwavering intensity, his invitation now brought to life in this secret confluence of art and yearning.

He had awaited her arrival in a secluded nook near the Turner, an island of privacy in a sea of artistic grandeur. His posture was one of casual elegance against the backdrop of gilded frames, yet his eyes betrayed a fervor that quickened Genevieve's pulse. As she approached, he offered a nod that bespoke both respect and something more—a silent acknowledgment of the step they were about to take beyond the boundaries of polite society.

"Lady Sinclair," he greeted her with a voice smooth as velvet, taking her gloved hand and bringing it to his lips. The contact was but a whisper, yet it resonated through her being like a peal of thunder. "Your presence honors both myself and the artisans whose work surrounds us."

His words struck Genevieve with force, stealing the breath from her lungs. She felt an inexplicable pull towards him, like a moth to flame—dangerous, yet irresistibly beautiful. "Lord Ravenswood," she managed to reply, her voice steady

CHAPTER TWELVE

despite the tumult within. "Your invitation was... unexpected."

The Marquess smiled then—a slow curve of his lips that seemed to promise secrets untold—and beckoned her forward. "And yet, you are here."

They moved through the gallery together, each step measured and deliberate. He spoke with an ease and eloquence that brought each piece to life, articulating thoughts on light and shadow that mirrored Genevieve's musings.

As they progressed from one masterpiece to another, their proximity became an unspoken dialogue in itself. Genevieve could feel the warmth emanating from him each time he leaned in to highlight a particular detail and could sense his gaze lingering on her when she contemplated a canvas.

"Tell me, Lady Sinclair," he murmured, his voice a velvet caress against the pounding of her heart, "is there not a certain beauty to be found in the forbidden? In seizing what society would deny us?"

Genevieve felt her breath catch in her throat at the Marquess's daring words. His question hung between them, heavy with unspoken implications that threatened the very boundaries of propriety she had been raised to uphold. Yet, as she met his gaze, an undeniable spark ignited deep within her—a longing to abandon decorum and surrender to the forbidden allure he presented.

"You speak dangerous truths, my Lord," she replied, her voice a hushed whisper amidst the gallery's hushed reverence. "Society's strictures are a gilded cage, and yet..." She trailed off, her eyes drawn to the star-crossed lovers immortalized on canvas before them.

The Marquess leaned nearer, his voice a low rumble that seemed to reverberate through her very being. "And yet, you cannot deny the yearning that stirs within you—the desire to shatter those confines and taste the freedom denied to us by birth and rank."

Genevieve's cheeks flushed, her composure wavering beneath his penetrating gaze. "Such words border on impropriety, my Lord," she scolded, though the breathlessness of her tone betrayed the effect his words had upon her.

A subtle smirk played upon the Marquess's lips as if he could sense the chink forming in her armor. "Impropriety?" he echoed, his tone rich with challenge. "Or merely the truth, spoken without fear of consequence?"

He took a step closer, invading her space with a boldness that sent Genevieve's pulse quickening. "Look into my eyes, Lady Sinclair, and tell me you do not feel the weight of societal shackles upon your very soul."

CHAPTER TWELVE

Genevieve found herself trapped by his gaze, those dark eyes seeming to lay bare the innermost desires she had long kept buried. She parted her lips to respond but found her voice had fled, leaving only a weighted silence that hung between them like a tangible force.

The Marquess reached out, his gloved fingers grazing the curve of her jaw with a featherlight touch that blazed through Genevieve like wildfire. "I see the truth reflected in your eyes," he murmured, his thumb tracing the swell of her bottom lip. "You may don the mask of propriety, but beneath beats the heart of a woman who yearns to be unchained."

A tremor ran through Genevieve at his bold caress, her carefully cultivated poise crumbling under the onslaught of his seduction. She knew she should withdraw, should rebuke his advances, and preserve what remained of her composure. Yet, some primal part of her was awakening, drawn like a moth to the flame of his forbidden allure.

"You speak in riddles, my Lord," she managed, though the words emerged breathless, lacking their intended conviction.

The Marquess chuckled, a low, rumbling sound that seemed to reverberate through her very core. "No riddles, my Lady," he countered, his fingers trailing along the slender column of her neck. "Merely the truth laid bare—a truth you know resides within your heart, no matter how fervently you may try to deny it."

Genevieve's resolve was crumbling; the walls she had so carefully constructed to guard her from temptation were now lying in shattered ruin at her feet. The Marquess's words, his touch, his very presence—all conspired to awaken a longing so primal, so fierce, that she found herself powerless to resist.

As his lips curved into a knowing smile, she knew he could see the naked desire reflected in her eyes—the defeat of her innocence at the hands of his seduction. And though every lesson ingrained by society screamed at her to flee, Genevieve found herself utterly entranced, drawn inexorably into the Marquess's web of sin and seduction.

Despite her will to be seduced by his presence alone, Genevieve tried every attempt at disguising her emotions. She averted her gaze when their eyes met, feigning an intent study of the brushwork before them. Yet beneath her practiced composure, her heart raced with a yearning she could scarcely contain.

The Marquess, too, was engulfed by Genevieve's presence and the fact that she accepted his invitation. He drank in every nuance of her being—the gentle rise and fall of her bosom, the delicate flush upon her cheeks, the curious tilt of her head as she contemplated each artwork. Though schooled in matters of society, he found himself unraveling in her orbit.

"Might I offer my interpretation, my Lady?" His voice was low, conspiratorial, as he stepped nearer. Genevieve felt the heat of his proximity like a searing brand yet managed a nod, her lips parting with a silent invitation.

The Marquess and Genevieve weaved through the crowds of the art gallery patrons, his words like whispered poetry caressing the shell of her ear. He spoke of the masterpieces surrounding them, and yet his tone hinted at deeper truths —of the beauty found in defiance, of the bravery inherent in pursuing one's passions without regard for propriety.

With each measured stride, the space between them seemed to grow thinner and more charged until Genevieve could feel the thrum of his presence like a tangible force. When he paused before a portrait depicting star-crossed lovers, his gaze found hers with an intensity that stole her breath.

The world seemed to contract until it consisted only of them and the art that spoke volumes in hushed tones—a symphony for their ears alone. Her heart began its silent rhythm in response to his closeness; she felt seen in ways that transcended mere physical observation.

It was then that he drew her aside into an alcove draped with heavy velvet curtains—a space removed from potential prying eyes. His fingers traced the line of her jaw with reverence, tilting her face towards his as he closed the distance between them.

"Genevieve," he breathed out, her name an invocation as his lips descended upon hers. The kiss was not one born merely out of desire but out of recognition—the kindling recognition of two souls reaching for one another across societal divides.

A conflagration erupted within Genevieve at his touch; passion unfurled like blooms under spring's first sun. The Marquess's arms encircled her with possessive tenderness as their mouths moved together in a dance as old as time.

In this secluded corner surrounded by expressions of beauty and passion immortalized on canvas, Genevieve surrendered to the moment. She gave herself over to the embrace, to the kiss that sealed her fate. Here in this temple dedicated to artistry and human emotion, she acknowledged what had been slowly dawning on her heart: she loved this man—this enigmatic figure shrouded in whispers and scandal—with every fiber of her being.

With each heartbeat that thundered in unison with his own, Genevieve understood that this love was not one she could—or would—deny or hideaway. It was fierce and bold; it demanded recognition regardless of consequence.

CHAPTER TWELVE

As they finally parted lips, breathless and with eyes locked onto each other's, there was no turning back. For Lady Genevieve Sinclair knew then that whatever path lay ahead would be one, she walked hand in hand with the Marquess —the man who had captured her heart irrevocably.

Thirteen

Genevieve sat at her writing desk, her thoughts still swirling with the intoxicating memory of her clandestine rendezvous with the Marquess. The warmth of his embrace, the passion in his kiss, and the depth of their connection had left an indelible mark upon her heart. She felt as though she had finally discovered her true path, a love that transcended the superficial confines of society's expectations.

A gentle rap on the door stirred Genevieve from her reverie. "Come in," she called, setting down her pen and turning to face the visitor.

Miss Charlotte burst into the room, her cheeks flushed with excitement and her eyes sparkling with the promise of juicy gossip. "Oh, Vivie, you'll never believe the whispers

I've just overheard!" she exclaimed, her words tumbling forth in a breathless torrent.

Genevieve leaned forward, her curiosity piqued by her friend's animated demeanor. "Do tell, Charlotte. What has the *ton* been buzzing about now?"

Charlotte took a seat on the edge of Genevieve's bed, her hands clasped together in eager anticipation. "It seems our charming Viscount Hartfield has been harboring a most scandalous secret," she revealed, her voice dropping to a conspiratorial whisper.

Genevieve felt a chill run down her spine, a sense of trepidation mingling with the thrill of impending revelation. "What secret could tarnish the Viscount's polished reputation?" she asked, her heart racing.

Charlotte leaned in closer, her eyes wide with the weight of her discovery. "The Viscount, for all his cultivated airs and graces, had fathered a child out of wedlock," she disclosed, her words hanging heavy in the air between them. "The result of a dalliance from his past, with a woman of questionable repute."

Genevieve gasped, her hand flying to her mouth in shock. The Viscount, the very man who had so ardently pursued her affections, had been concealing such a scandalous truth. She felt a wave of emotions wash over her—disbelief, disappointment, and a strange sense of relief.

CHAPTER THIRTEEN

"The mother now threatens to come forward and demand that her son be acknowledged," Charlotte continued, her voice tinged with a mix of excitement and concern. "If she does, it will shatter the Viscount's carefully constructed facade and ruin him in the eyes of society." She drew a quick breath before concluding, "Did the Viscount propose?"

As the weight of this revelation settled upon her, Genevieve felt a profound sense of clarity. The Viscount's polished exterior, which had once captivated her, now lay in tatters, exposing the harsh reality that he was a man beholden to his indiscretions and the consequences thereof.

In that moment, Genevieve's resolve solidified. She knew, with unwavering certainty, that her future did not lie with the Viscount. Her heart belonged to the Marquess—a man who, despite his rumored transgressions, had shown her a depth of character and vulnerability that transcended the shallow confines of society's expectations.

Genevieve drew in a deep breath, steeling herself against the weight of Charlotte's revelations. "The Viscount and I were never engaged, my dear friend," she confessed, her voice low and tinged with a hint of remorse. "Though there were whispers and speculations, the truth is far more complicated."

Charlotte leaned forward, her eyes wide with rapt attention, silently urging Genevieve to continue her confession.

"That night, in the garden," Genevieve began, her fingers idly tracing the delicate embroidery on her shawl, "it was not a romantic tryst but rather a result of a heated exchange when the Viscount spotted me speaking with the Marquess." She paused, gathering her thoughts before continuing. "The Viscount's charms turned entitled, and in a moment of weakness, I allowed him to steal a kiss."

Charlotte gasped, her hand flying to her mouth in shock. "Vivie! How utterly scandalous!" she exclaimed, her voice a mixture of surprise and delight at this juicy revelation.

Genevieve nodded solemnly, her cheeks flushing with a mix of shame and defiance. "I know it was improper, but I allowed it, and now I feel remorse."

Charlotte leaned back, her expression a blend of concern and curiosity. "But surely the Viscount did not merely seek to tarnish your virtue?" she probed, her brow furrowed. "Did he not intend to make you an offer of marriage?"

Genevieve shook her head, a rueful smile playing upon her lips. "Alas, my dear Charlotte, the Viscount's intentions were far more base than that. He sought only to claim a fleeting conquest, to add another notch to his bedpost before moving on to his next pursuit."

Charlotte's eyes widened in disbelief, and she let out a low whistle. "The scoundrel!" she exclaimed, her hands balling into fists at her sides. "To think he would deceive you so, preying upon your innocent affections for his own selfish gains."

Genevieve placed a calming hand on her friend's arm, her expression one of weary acceptance. "While his actions were indeed reprehensible, I cannot fault him entirely," she admitted. "For I, too, allowed myself to be swayed by desires that defied the boundaries of propriety."

Charlotte regarded her friend with a mix of sympathy and admiration. "But you had the strength to resist his advances, did you not?" she asked, her voice laced with concern.

Genevieve nodded, her resolve unwavering. "Indeed, I did."

WITH A STEADY HAND and clarity of purpose, Genevieve pens a letter to Viscount Hartfield, her words flowing from a wellspring of newfound strength and self-assurance. She bids him a final farewell, revealing the truth about his past indiscretions and the existence of his illegitimate offspring.

Genevieve's quill danced across the parchment, each meticulously penned word a testament to the transformation within her soul. No longer was she the meek debutante, beholden to society's expectations; she was a woman encouraged by the truth and fortified by her newfound love.

My Lord,

Your actions, though veiled in the trappings of gentility, have proven you a man unworthy of the esteem you so ardently seek. The existence of your natural child, born of impropriety, stands as a testament to the hollowness of your character—a truth I can no longer ignore.

Let this letter serve as an unequivocal severing of any bond that may have existed between us. Your actions have laid bare the hollowness of your character, and I cannot, in good conscience, continue to entertain the notion of aligning my future with one whose past is so tainted by deceit.

Lady Genevieve Sinclair

CHAPTER THIRTEEN

Genevieve paused for a moment, memories of their stolen moments flitting through her mind like phantoms—the whispered poetry, the lingering glances, the intoxicating kiss that had once set her heart aflame. Yet, those recollections now rang hollow, stripped of their allure by the harsh light of truth.

As she seals the letter with a flourish of wax, Genevieve feels a profound sense of liberation. She has broken free from the shackles of societal expectations and the allure of superficial charm, choosing instead to embrace a love that is built upon a foundation of honesty, vulnerability, and a meeting of souls.

With a resolute nod, she summons a footman. She instructs him to deliver the letter posthaste, severing her ties to the Viscount and clearing the path for her future with the Marquess—a future that, though fraught with its challenges and uncertainties, promises a depth of passion and fulfillment that she had once thought unattainable.

As the footman departs, Genevieve turns her gaze toward the window, watching as the clouds roll in.

Fourteen

The steady patter of rain against the window pane provides a melancholic soundtrack to Genevieve's musings as she gazes out at the dreary night. Her thoughts are a whirlwind of anticipation and trepidation, her heart still racing from the memory of the Marquess's searing kiss and the realization that she has irrevocably chosen him over the Viscount.

A discreet knock at the door breaks her reverie, and she turns to find her maid, a look of bewilderment upon her face. "My lady," the young woman whispers, "the Marquess of Ravenswood has arrived downstairs through the kitchen —he has requested a private audience."

Genevieve's breath catches in her throat as she processes this bold and unprecedented move by the Marquess. Propriety dictates that she should refuse him, for to receive an unaccompanied gentleman would be the height of scandal. Yet, the yearning in her heart overrides all sense of decorum, and she finds herself nodding, instructing the maid to show him to her private sitting room.

Moments later, she descends the stairs, her heart thundering in her chest as she opens the door to see the Marquess's imposing figure. Without preamble, she takes his hand and leads him through a discreet side entrance, out into the rain-soaked gardens, and toward the stables—a place where they can converse without prying eyes or ears.

The rain intensifies as they hurry through the gardens, the wind whipping at their clothes. Genevieve can feel the Marquess's hand trembling in hers, and she squeezes it reassuringly. When they reach the stables, she fumbles with the lock, her fingers slick with rain. The Marquess steps forward, taking the key from her and deftly unlocking the door.

They step inside, and the heavy door swings shut behind them, plunging them into darkness. Genevieve fumbles for a candle, and soon, a warm glow illuminates the small space. The Marquess stands before her, his eyes gleaming with a mixture of anticipation and something more profound—a vulnerability that she has never seen before.

"My lady," he begins, his voice low and husky, "I could not stay away. I had to see you again."

Genevieve's heart leaps into her throat. "But it is improper," she protests, even as she steps closer to him.

"I do not care for propriety," the Marquess declares, his voice fierce. "I only care for you."

Genevieve's heart raced as she stood before the Marquess, his imposing presence filling the small stable with an electric tension. A war raged within her—the deeply ingrained sense of propriety battling against the undeniable longing that coursed through her veins.

For a fleeting moment, her mind drifted to the Viscount and the whispers of his indiscretion that had sundered their bond. *Was she destined to tread the same path, to become the subject of salacious gossip and scorn?* The notion sent a chill down her spine, a reminder of the unforgiving scrutiny under which she lived.

Yet, as her gaze met the Marquess's, any lingering doubt evaporated like morning mist; there was a depth in his eyes, a raw vulnerability that resonated with the very core of her being. In that moment, she knew—with every fiber of her existence—that this man held the key to her heart's desire, and she would risk everything for the chance to love him truly and without restraint.

The barriers of propriety seemed to crumble as she took a step closer, her hand reaching out to caress his weather-beaten cheek. The Marquess leaned into her, his eyes fluttering closed as if savoring the simple intimacy of her touch. Genevieve's breath caught in her throat, a heady mixture of fear and exhilaration coursing through her.

"My lord," she whispered, her voice trembling with the weight of her emotions, "I cannot deny what burns within me any longer. Society's rules, the constraints of my station—they pale in comparison to the fire that kindles in my soul when I am near you."

The Marquess's eyes opened, burning with an intensity that threatened to consume her. In a single, fluid motion, he gathered her into his embrace, his lips crashing against hers in a kiss that ignited every nerve ending in her body. Genevieve surrendered herself to the torrent of passion, her fingers tangling in his rain-drenched hair as she returned his ardor with equal fervor.

In that moment, the world beyond the stable ceased to exist. There was only the Marquess, his hands roaming the curves of her body, his lips trailing a blazing path along the column of her neck. Genevieve felt herself unraveling, the boundaries of propriety and decorum falling away like so many gossamer threads.

She knew, in that moment, that she would follow this man to the ends of the earth. She would defy the conventions of society, brave the whispers and sneers of the ton, for the chance to experience this all-consuming love that threatened to engulf her entirely. The Marquess was her destiny, her heart's true desire, and she would cling to him with every ounce of her being, consequences be damned.

As their kisses deepened, Genevieve felt a sense of liberation unlike anything she had ever known. The shackles of expectation and duty fell away, leaving her free to pursue the one thing she had yearned for her entire life —a love that transcended the rigid confines of her world and ignited her very soul.

The Marquess breaks apart from her. Breathing heavily, he began, "Genevieve," his voice barely more than a whisper now. He hesitated as if gathering the strength to unburden himself of a secret long held within. "There is something I must reveal to you, a truth that has haunted me for far too long."

Genevieve's heart raced, but she did not falter. She reached out, her hand finding him, and offered him an encouraging nod. The Marquess drew in a deep breath, and the words began to pour forth like water released from a dam.

He spoke of a duel, a tragic confrontation born of misplaced honor and pride, that had left another man lifeless upon the cold ground. The lady in question had lied about a liaison between them to hide the unborn child she had conceived by her footman. She was his childhood friend, and he felt the need to defend her against her husband, who would have beaten her or worse. The Marquess's eyes shone with a haunted anguish as he recounted the events that had transpired, the weight of his actions heavy upon his shoulders.

As Genevieve listened, she felt a deep well of compassion rise within her. She saw not the disgraced nobleman that society had painted him to be but a man tormented by the consequences of his choices. She understood now why he had been shunned, why whispers of scandal had followed him like a shadow.

"I cannot change the past," the Marquess confessed, his voice thick with emotion. "But I can strive to make amends, to live a life that honors the memory of the man I wronged."

Genevieve squeezed his hand, her heart swelling with love and admiration for this man who had bared his soul to her. She understood now the actual depth of his character, the strength, and resilience that lay beneath his brooding exterior.

"Whatever challenges lie ahead," she vowed, her voice steady and relentless, "I will face them by your side. Our love will be a beacon that guides us through even the darkest of storms."

In that sacred space, sheltered from the world and its judgments, a profound bond was forged between them. The rain continued to fall outside, a cleansing force that seemed to wash away the sins of the past and clear the way for a future written by their own hands, a life lived authentically and without regret.

The Marquess gazed deep into Genevieve's eyes, his features etched with an intensity that stirred her very soul. The shadows that danced across his face seemed to part, revealing a vulnerability she had never before witnessed. It was as if, in that moment, all pretense had fallen away, leaving only the raw, unguarded truth between them.

"Genevieve," he murmured, her name a reverent whisper upon his lips. "I fear I can no longer conceal the truth that burns within my heart." He drew in a steadying breath as if steeling himself for the weight of his confession.

Genevieve felt her pulse quicken, her body attuned to the gravity of the moment. She remained still, her eyes never leaving his, silently urging him to lay bare the depths of his feelings.

"I love you," the Marquess declared, his voice ringing with a conviction that resonated through the very air around them. "From the moment our paths first crossed, you have captured my heart and soul in a way I never thought possible."

A tremor of emotion swept through Genevieve, her fingers curling tightly around the Marquess's hand. She heard the sincerity in his words, saw the raw adoration that shone in his eyes, and knew that this was no fleeting infatuation.

This was a love that had taken root deep within him, a love that had weathered the storms of his past and bloomed anew in her presence.

"I have lived my life in the shadows, haunted by the specter of my own mistakes," the Marquess continued, his voice thick with emotion. "But you, my dearest Genevieve, have shown me the path to redemption, the promise of a future where love triumphs over the whispers of scandal and the chains of propriety."

Genevieve felt tears prick at the corners of her eyes, her heart swelling with a love so profound, so all-consuming, that it threatened to overwhelm her. This man, this enigmatic and passionate soul, had laid bare the depths of his devotion and, in doing so, had claimed a piece of her heart that she knew would forever be his.

Without a word, she reached up, her fingers tracing the contours of his face with a tenderness that spoke volumes. In that moment, no words were needed, for their love transcended the confines of mere speech. It was a language of the heart, a sacred bond that bound them together in a way that defied the constraints of society and the judgments of the world around them.

Fifteen

The Marquess's hands cradle Genevieve's face, his thumbs gently caressing her cheeks as they share a kiss that speaks of a love untamed by societal constraints. The intensity of their connection sends a shiver down her spine, and she clings to him as if to anchor herself amidst the whirlwind of emotions that threaten to sweep her away.

As they break apart, Genevieve gazes into the depths of the Marquess's eyes, her own brimming with unshed tears. "I never imagined I could feel this way," she whispers, her voice barely audible above the pattern of rain against the stable roof. "My heart has been awakened, and I fear it will never be the same."

The Marquess smiles, a tender expression softening the

hard lines of his face. "Nor will mine, my love," he replies, his voice husky with emotion.

Enveloped in the safety of each other's arms, Genevieve and the Marquess surrendered to the overwhelming force of their love. With tender reverence, he undressed her, the rustle of fabric and the gentle pitter-patter of raindrops on the stable roof providing a soothing symphony to their intimate dance.

His fingers traced the curve of her shoulder, lingering on the delicate lace of her gown before deftly unfastening the row of buttons. As the fabric pooled at her waist, he took a moment to admire the beauty of her exposed form, the pale lantern filtering through the wooded beams casting a soft glow upon her skin.

Genevieve, in turn, reached for the Marquess's shirt, her trembling hands working to free the buttons from their moorings. With each inch of exposed skin, she marveled at the strength and power contained within his muscular frame, her heart swelling with love and desire.

Their eyes locked, a silent conversation passing between them as they continued to undress one another. The air around them crackled with electricity, the anticipation building with each passing moment.

Finally, they stood before each other, naked and vulnerable, their bodies bathed in the ethereal light of the lantern. The

CHAPTER FIFTEEN

Marquess lowered himself onto the soft hay, pulling Genevieve into his embrace as they lay entwined in each other's arms.

The Marquess's eyes devoured the sight of Genevieve's naked form; he marveled at the curves and contours of her figure, each line and shape a testament to her femininity and grace.

His hands, seemingly of their own accord, began to explore the landscape of her body, tracing the delicate lines of her collarbone before wandering down to the swell of her breasts. The warmth of his touch sent a shiver down her spine, and she arched her back, offering herself to him in a silent plea for more.

The Marquess obliged, his fingers gently squeezing and caressing her breasts as his mouth found the sensitive peak of one nipple. He teased the tight bud with his tongue, flicking and swirling until Genevieve gasped with pleasure, her fingers tangling in his hair as she held him close.

His other hand continued its exploration, drifting down her side and over the curve of her hip before coming to rest on the soft flesh of her inner thigh. He could feel the heat radiating from her core, and he knew that she was as consumed by desire as he was.

With a low growl, the Marquess shifted his position, his mouth leaving her breast to trail kisses down her stomach and along the sensitive skin of her inner thigh. Genevieve's breath hitched as she felt his hot breath against her most intimate parts, and she knew that she was on the precipice of something truly extraordinary.

The Marquess's fingers began to work their magic, teasing and stroking her until she was writhing beneath him, her body trembling with the force of her desire. He watched her face, drinking in the pleasure that washed over her features as he brought her closer and closer to the edge.

As Genevieve's cries of ecstasy filled the stable, the Marquess knew that he had never felt anything so pure and so powerful in his entire life. He had been a fool ever to think that he could resist the pull of her love, and he vowed to spend the rest of his days cherishing and protecting her.

With one final, exquisite touch, the Marquess sent Genevieve over the edge, her body convulsing with the force of her release as she cried out his name. He held her close, his own body trembling with the force of his emotions as he whispered words of love and devotion into her ear.

As the waves of pleasure subsided, Genevieve looked up at the Marquess, her eyes shining with love and gratitude. She knew that she had found her soulmate, the one person who truly understood and cherished her for who she was.

Gently, he kissed her forehead, his lips lingering on her skin as he whispered a promise that he knew he would keep for all eternity. "I love you, Genevieve," he murmured, his voice thick with emotion. "And I will never let you go."

Their bodies melded together, the heat of their skin a stark contrast to the cool night air. The Marquess's hands roamed her body once more, each touch eliciting a shiver of pleasure that coursed through her veins. Genevieve responded in kind, her fingers exploring the contours of his chest, the ridges of his abdomen, and the strength of his arms.

As their passion reached a fever pitch, the Marquess entered her, their bodies moving in perfect harmony. Each thrust was a testament to their love, a physical manifestation of the connection that bound them together.

Genevieve clung to him, her nails digging into the flesh of his back as she surrendered herself to the overwhelming sensations that threatened to consume her. The Marquess, in turn, held her close, his breath hot against her neck as he whispered words of love and devotion.

Their movements grew more urgent, their breaths coming in ragged gasps as they raced toward the precipice of release. With a final, desperate thrust, they reached the peak of their passion, their bodies shuddering in unison as they succumbed to the overwhelming power of their love.

As the waves of pleasure subsided, Genevieve and the Marquess lay entwined in each other's arms, their hearts beating in tandem. The sound of the rain continued to fall around them, a gentle reminder of the world outside their sanctuary.

For a moment, they held each other, their bodies slick with sweat and their breaths slowly returning to normal. The intimacy of their union had transcended the physical, forging a bond that could never be broken.

As the first rays of dawn began to break through the darkness, Genevieve and the Marquess reluctantly parted, their bodies weary but their hearts full. They dressed in silence, each lost in their own thoughts as they prepared to face the challenges that lay ahead.

"Marry me, Genevieve," the Marquess whispered, his eyes shining with unshed tears of joy. "Be my wife, my partner, my everything. Let us face the world together, united in our love and unwavering in our commitment to one another."

With a radiant smile, Genevieve responded with a single, heartfelt word: "Yes."

As the Marquess held Genevieve close, her heart swelled with a love that transcended the boundaries of her world. She knew that the path ahead would not be an easy one, that they would face challenges and obstacles that would test the very foundation of their love. But she also knew that, together, they could weather any storm, that their love was a beacon that would guide them through even the darkest of nights.

The Marquess gently brushed a stray lock of hair from Genevieve's face, his touch a tender caress that sent shivers of delight down her spine. "My love," he murmured, his voice a low rumble that seemed to resonate deep within her soul. "I promise to cherish and protect you, to honor and adore you for all the days of my life."

Genevieve's heart fluttered at his words, a maelstrom of emotions swirling within her. "I avow to cherish and revere you," Genevieve responded, her voice quivering with the weight of her sentiments. "I will be your helpmate, your intimate, your pillar. As one, we will confront any trials ahead, bonded in our devotion and unbending in our pledge to each other."

The Marquess leaned in, his lips brushing against Genevieve's in a tender kiss that seemed to seal their vows. As they lost themselves in the sweetness of the moment, the world around them faded away, leaving only the two of them entwined in a love that would last for all eternity.

Epilogue

SEVEN YEARS LATER

The soft morning light filtered through the lace curtains, bathing the bedchamber in a warm, golden glow. Genevieve stirred beneath the downy sheets, her eyes fluttering open to take in the familiar surroundings of her sanctuary—the Marquess's estate in the lush Yorkshire countryside.

A contented smile played upon her lips as she rolled over, her gaze settling upon the slumbering form of her beloved husband, the Marquess of Ravenswood. Even in repose, his features held a rugged handsomeness that never failed to stir her heart. Seven years had passed since their fateful wedding day, and yet the intensity of her love for him burned as bright as ever.

As if sensing her adoring gaze, the Marquess's eyes slowly opened, his lips curving into a tender smile. "Good morning, my love," he murmured, his voice still husky with sleep as he reached out to caress her cheek.

Genevieve leaned into his touch, reveling in the familiar warmth and strength of his calloused fingers. "Good morning, my darling," she replied, her eyes sparkling with contentment.

A soft giggle from the adjoining room caught her attention, and she turned in time to see their four young children tumbling through the door, their faces alight with mischievous grins. Genevieve's heart swelled with maternal love as she watched them clamber onto the bed, surrounding their parents in a tangle of tiny limbs and joyful laughter.

"Mama! Papa!" the eldest, a precocious girl of six, exclaimed. "We're awake!"

Genevieve's gaze swept over her brood, her heart swelling with a profound sense of pride and fulfillment. Amidst the tangle of cherubic faces, she could scarcely believe the abundance of blessings that had been bestowed upon her.

First, there was Isabelle, her eldest—a spirited young lady with eyes as blue as the summer sky and hair the color of burnished copper. Even at her tender age, Isabelle possessed an inquisitive mind and a zest for adventure that reminded Genevieve so much of herself. Next came the twins, Lydia and Sophia, their identical faces framed by dark curls and lit up with infectious grins. Though only five, their mischievous antics kept the household in a constant state of joyful chaos.

And then, her eyes settled upon her youngest, the son she had so desperately longed for—Edward, the precious babe who would one day inherit his father's esteemed title. At a mere three years old, his cherubic countenance and clear, brown eyes held an endearing innocence that never failed to melt Genevieve's heart. As she watched him fall into the Marquess's embrace, she was reminded of the incredible journey that had led her to this moment—a journey marked by heartache, defiance, and an unwavering determination to forge her own path.

It was Edward's birth that had secured not only the continuation of the Ravenswood lineage but also the preservation of Genevieve's own family legacy. With no male heir to inherit the Sinclair peerage, her father's title and estates would have been lost to history. Yet, by the grace of providence, Edward's arrival had ensured that the Sinclair name would endure, his birthright as the future Lord Sinclair safeguarding the heritage that had once seemed so precarious.

The Marquess chuckled, gathering their children into his strong embrace. "So I see, my little rascals," he teased, dropping a kiss onto each of their tousled heads.

As Genevieve looked around at her little family, a profound sense of gratitude washed over her. For so long, she had feared that the constraints of society and the weight of reputation would forever bar her from true happiness. Yet here she was, surrounded by the unconditional love and joy that she had once thought unattainable.

Her gaze met the Marquess's, and in that silent exchange, she saw the depth of his love reflected back at her—a love that had withstood the tests of time and the scrutiny of the ton. Together, they had forged a life built upon the foundations of trust, vulnerability, and an unwavering commitment to one another.

With a tender smile, Genevieve pulled her family close, basking in the warmth of their embrace. The path to this moment had been fraught with challenges and uncertainties, but every trial and every heartache had been worth it to find herself here, in the loving arms of her soulmate and their beautiful children.

THE END

Acknowledgments

"Childe Harold's Pilgrimage"
"She Walks in Beauty"
Lord Byron

J. M. W. Turner
Painter

Win the Heart of the Duchess

THE THUNDERBOLT SERIES - BOOK 3

Juliet, the Duchess of Wrotham, a captivating widow trapped in a gilded cage, yearns for a life filled with laughter and the promise of a child. But the relentless whispers of time mock her dreams. Then, a chance encounter with the enigmatic **Duke of Ashbourne** awakens a forbidden desire. As notorious as he is handsome, Ashbourne carries the weight of a scandal that ostracizes him from society. Yet, beneath his brooding exterior lies a wounded soul yearning for connection.

Drawn together by a powerful yearning, Juliet and Ashbourne embark on a passionate affair, their love a defiance of societal expectations. But the whispers of Ashbourne's past refuse to remain silent. As Juliet delves deeper, can she see beyond the rumors and trust the man behind them? Will their love withstand the relentless scrutiny of the ton, or will the truth of his bygone transgressions shatter their fragile bond?

The Thunderbolt Series - Book 3
by Trisha Fuentes
Ebook & Paperback

Your Next Series
SERVICE DAUGHTER SERIES

HARDSHIP SHOULDN'T HAVE TO BE SUCH AN UPHILL BATTLE

Meet Louisa, Caroline & Hannah

Three daughters were born into service. Each has their own story to tell and happily ever after. Simple, ordinary, and untitled, unnoticed by the wealthy, struggling with how to survive, how to obtain joy...much less a husband.

YOUR NEXT SERIES

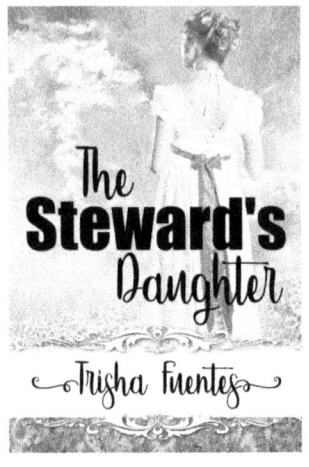

ALL LOUISA WANTED WAS TO BE USEFUL...

The only child of Mr. Ralph Hadley, Land Steward to the Earl of Monbossom, Miss Louisa Hadley lives in a small cottage on the Monbossom estate with her father. When she accidentally breaks her foot after dismounting a horse she is forced to stay in the main house while her father tends to the Earl abroad. With the family now responsible for Louisa's well-being, the classes have reversed as Louisa is constantly scorned by her friends in service. Her circumstances take a more dramatic turn when she stumbles upon the Earl of Monbossom while saving a duckling.

When did he return from France? And who knew his eyes were so blue?

Book 1
Available in paperback & ebook

CAN A KITCHEN MAID FIND TRUE HAPPINESS?

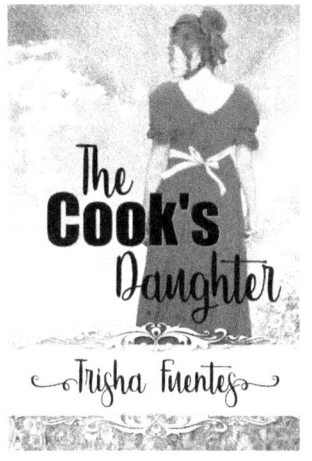

Miss Caroline Bates began working in the kitchen with her mother when she was twelve. Caroline grew up with the children of Wellsbury Hall, and watched Lord Gretner's eldest son, Alfred court several noblewomen until one day he finds Caroline practically naked in a nearby moor river.

Is Caroline ruined for all eternity or does she use this mischance to her advantage?

Book 2
Available in paperback & ebook

YOUR NEXT SERIES

WHICH PATH TO FOLLOW?

The only daughter of a curator of St. Anne's Church, Miss Hannah Pickering, grew up knowing she was going to become a nun until she was introduced to one of her father's parishioners. Tempted by the handsome widower who attends her father's church, Hannah is suddenly forced to make a worrisome decision.

Book 3
Available in paperback & ebook

The Family Fix

HOT NEW AUTHOR!

TIRED OF BEING THE SINGLE ONE AT FAMILY GATHERINGS?

Isabella Santos is a rising star architect with no time for love. But when her family's relentless matchmaking reaches a fever pitch, she needs a plan. Enter **Rafael Torres**, her cousin's charming best friend. A fake relationship is the perfect solution.

The problem is that pretending to be in love is a lot easier said than done.

As sparks fly and their charade heats up, Isabella and Rafael find themselves blurring the lines between pretend and reality. Can they navigate meddling families, hidden desires, and the thrill of a love that wasn't supposed to happen?

A Fake Relationship Romance

by Mia Munoz

Ebook & Paperback

About Trisha

Hey, it's Trish...

I'm a Romance Author of 34+ books, plus an Indie Book Publisher of 48+ Pen Name Authors.

I've been writing romance with a whole lot of heat lately. I love to write fun, fast romances with witty leading ladies getting that gorgeous, sexy, yet lovable guy that doesn't take months to finish. Happily Ever After with a little bit of love angst in between. Whether you yearn for Historical or Modern, I always have a story for you!

Rejoice, Romance Reader...

For upcoming releases, book news, and other goodies, subscribe to my Newsletter!
https://mailchi.mp/567874a61a56/aab-landing-page

- instagram.com/authortrish
- amazon.com/Trisha-Fuentes/e/B002BME1MI
- facebook.com/booksbyTrish
- youtube.com/theardentartist

Also by Trisha Fuentes

✸ Modern Romance ✸

A Sacrifice Play

Faded Dreams

Never Say Forever

✸ Historical ✸

The Anzan Heir

Magnet & Steele

The Relentless Rogue

One Starry Night

In The Moonlight With You

Captivating the Captain

The Merry Widow

Unrequited Love

The Summer Romance of the Duke

✻ Series ✻

HOLLINGER

Dare To Love - Book 1

A Matchless Match - Book 2

Arrogance & Conceit - Book 3

Impropriety - Book 4

SERVICE • DAUGHTER

The Steward's Daughter - Book 1

The Cook's Daughter - Book 2

The Curator's Daughter - Book 3

THUNDERBOLT

The Surprise Heir - Book 1

A Dance of Deception - Book 2

Win the Heart of a Duchess- Book 3

OBSESSION

Unsuitable Obsession - Part One

Broken Obsession - Part Two

ESCAPE

Swept Away - Book 1

Fire & Rescue - Book 2

The Domain King - Book 3

AGE · GAP · ROMANCE

Whispers of Yesterday - Book 1

His Encore, Her Ecstasy - Book 2

Against the Wind - Book 3

www.ingramcontent.com/pod-product-compliance
Lightning Source LLC
LaVergne TN
LVHW021824060526
838201LV00058B/3497